# A Gift from the Boys

*Books by Art Buchwald:*

A GIFT FROM THE BOYS

THE BRAVE COWARD

ART BUCHWALD'S PARIS

Vasiliu

# A Gift̰̰̰̰̰̰̰̰
# from the Boys

by

*Art Buchwald,* 1925-

HARPER & BROTHERS, PUBLISHERS, NEW YORK

~~~~~~~~~~~~~~~~

And then they tell the story about the lion walking through the jungle. He met a giraffe and said to him, "Giraffe, who is the king of the jungle?"

The giraffe quivered and said, "You are, oh mighty lion. No one but you."

Satisfied, the lion walked a little further and ran into a buffalo.

"Who is the king of the jungle?" he roared.

"You are, lion," the buffalo replied. "You're the king of the jungle."

Ten minutes later the lion saw a group of monkeys in a tree.

Before he could even ask the question they yelled, "The lion is the king of the jungle."

Later on he met an elephant. "Elephant," the lion said, "who is the king of the jungle?"

The elephant picked the lion up with his trunk and threw him against a tree. Then the elephant went over and gave the lion a series of harsh kicks. Then, after sitting on him for moments and giving him one final mauling, the elephant ambled away.

After he had gone, the bedraggled lion picked himself off the ground and said, "He just doesn't know—he just doesn't know."

~~~~~~~~~~~~~~~~

# A Gift from the Boys

# 1

THE Bay of Naples looked beautiful in the early-morning light. I hadn't slept much, thinking of Karen, and I had packed the previous night so there wasn't much for me to do except stand on the deck of the S.S. *Continentale* and watch the ship pull into port. Frank Bartlett and William joined me as I leaned over the rail.

"It doesn't look bad from here," I said.

"Anything looks good after this tub," Bartlett growled.

Karen, wearing her mink coat and a brand-new hat, ran over to where we were standing and said excitedly. "Isn't it gorgeous? Where's Rome?"

"You can't see it from here," I told her. "It's a hundred and forty miles behind those mountains."

"I'm so excited," she said. "I want to thank you gentlemen for everything. I hope when you get to Rome you look me up."

"Who said you were going to Rome?" William asked.

"Well, I assumed once I got to Italy I could go where I wanted."

"Don't go making any decisions on your own," William said. "We're going to stay at the Excelsior in Naples to-night, and we'll decide who does what tomorrow morning."

Karen looked at Bartlett but he didn't say anything.

I winked at Karen, but she seemed too distraught to notice me.

We were all leaning over the rail watching as the ship approached the harbor when a motor launch came along-side the *Continentale*'s ladder. One civilian and two uni-formed policemen jumped from the launch to the ship. We didn't pay any attention to them, but a few minutes later the three men plus a ship's officer came marching toward us.

"That's him," said the officer, pointing to Bartlett.

The civilian saluted halfheartedly. "Signor Bartelini," he began.

"The name's Bartlett. Frank Bartlett.

"Our records say your name is Bartelini. That's a good Italian name."

"Look, mister," Bartlett said, "I'm not Italian. I'm Ameri-can. Who the hell are you, anyway?"

"I'm Inspector Ruffino of the Italian Security Police. My branch is under orders from the Ministry of the In-terior to take your American passport and confiscate it."

"I'm not giving up my passport to anybody. You're going to have to take it from me."

The Inspector motioned to the two uniformed police-men, who stepped forward. William jumped between them and Bartlett.

2

Bartlett said, "Hold it, William. Okay, Inspector. How much?"

"How much what?"

"One hundred bucks, two hundred bucks? You're holding all the cards."

"Signor Bartelini, I don't want a bribe. I just want your passport. Please give it to me."

The policeman moved forward again. Bartlett wet his lips, took out the passport and handed it over.

Karen handed hers over too.

The Inspector looked at it a moment and then returned it. "I don't want yours. You are an American citizen."

"I am too," Bartlett said.

"Signor Bartelini, in the eyes of the Italian Government you are a deportee . . . that is to say, a deportee of Italian birth. Because you were born in Sicily, the United States, after making you what you are, has forced us to take you back. We are not any happier about it than you are. But since you have been forced upon us, you will be treated as an Italian, subject to Italian laws and responsible to Italian officials. We are aware you had some social standing in the United States as a leading racketeer, but to us you are just another national. If you don't obey our laws, we will put you in confinement, and, I assure you, our prisons are not up to American standards."

"Okay, okay," said Bartlett. "Forget the sermon. I've got to catch a boat for Capri."

"Capri is off limits to you, Signor Bartelini."

"Off limits?"

"So are Rome and Florence, Genoa and Venice. As a

matter of fact, the entire mainland is off limits."

"Where am I supposed to go?"

The Inspector took a piece of paper out of his pocket. "I believe you understand Italian?"

"Yeah," Bartlett said.

The Inspector started reading in Italian. "Frank Bartelini, by direction of the Minister of the Interior, you are to proceed to La Coma, Sicily, the place of your birth, and you are confined to the limits of this town until otherwise authorized. If you leave La Coma without written permission, you will be violating Italian law and will be subject to fine and imprisonment. You will be required to report twice a week to the carabinieri of the La Coma district, and you are forbidden under any conditions to have contact with other deportees. This order goes into effect immediately. You will be delivered to La Coma by police authorities."

The Inspector folded the paper.

"What did he say?" William asked.

Bartlett looked as if he was in a trance. "He said I'd have to return to La Coma, where I was born."

"He's nuts," William said.

Bartlett snapped to William, "Call the American Ambassador right away."

Inspector Ruffino said, "I'm afraid you won't find the American Ambassador very helpful. He is quite embarrassed about the problem of deportees."

"Inspector," said Bartlett, "I know you've got a job to do and I appreciate it. But you can't send me back to my home town. I left there as a baby. I don't know anybody there. I'll make a deal with you. Let me stay here in Naples like Luciano. I promise I won't cause any trouble. I'm not going to be in Italy more than a month."

"It isn't up to me," Ruffino replied. "It's up to the Minister of the Interior and he's decided to have you sent to La Coma."

"I'll give you five thousand bucks in cash. Be a sport."

"I'm sorry, but you have to go to La Coma."

Karen said, "Well, I know one thing. I'm not going to Sicily."

"Shut up," said William. "The boss is trying to think."

The ship docked a half hour later and the tiresome business of customs began. Inspector Ruffino and his two uniformed policemen stayed close to our party.

The Italian customs chief went down the line marking everyone's luggage with a piece of chalk. He didn't ask anyone to open his bag. But when he got to Bartlett he stopped. I saw Ruffino wink at the customs man.

"Have you anything to declare?" the chief asked Bartlett.

"No," said Bartlett.

"Please open all your bags."

"You didn't open anybody else's bags."

"Please. All the bags."

While William opened the suitcases and the steamer trunk, the customs man continued down the line marking bags without questioning anyone. He finally came back to us.

Bartlett must have had at least twenty suits in his steamer trunk, forty shirts, and God knows how many pairs of shoes.

He had silk underwear and silk pajamas all initialed

5

"F.B." He also must have had fifty ties.

Besides the clothes, he had a full set of golf clubs.

The customs official had no respect for the expensive clothes and tore through the bags, throwing them in all directions.

"Hey," said William. "Be careful what you're doing."

"Who are you?" the chief asked.

"I'm his valet," William replied.

"Valet," sneered the customs man, shoving and pulling the clothes.

"Where's the head of customs?" Bartlett demanded.

"I'm the head of customs," the official replied.

"Well, it's a hell of a way to encourage tourists."

"You're not a tourist," the official replied. "What is this?"

"It's a portable radio," Bartlett replied. "It's personal property."

"It looks new to me. The tag is still on it. And what is this?"

The chief held up a Polaroid camera.

"It's my personal camera.

"It's new and you didn't declare it."

"I didn't know you had to declare your own camera."

The chief said, waving his hands, "He didn't know! He didn't know! You're an Italian citizen. You have to declare everything."

"I'm not an Italian citizen. I'm an American," Bartlett yelled.

"Where is your American passport?" the chief yelled back.

"He's got it," Bartlett said, pointing to Ruffino.

"It's void," Ruffino replied.

The chief took out a pad of paper and started writing on it. "You're being fined for not declaring the radio and the camera. The fine is double the value of both items, which comes to . . ." He referred to a book. "To . . . 208,900 lire."

"I don't have any lire," Bartlett said.

"We'll take dollars," the chief said. "Please come over to the cashier."

While Bartlett was taken over to pay the fine, William tried to put the clothes back in some semblance of order. I said to Inspector Ruffino, "You guys play pretty rough."

"Who are you?" he asked.

I gave him my card. "I'm just a newspaperman along for the ride."

Ruffino looked at it and said to me, "We don't like deportees. If you make gangsters out of people, you have no right to send them back to us. Write that in your newspaper."

"I might do that," I said.

William ordered a porter to take the bags to a taxi.

Karen said to the customs official, "What do you want me to open, General?"

The customs official smiled and looked approvingly at Karen. "Nothing, Signorina. The only thing I ask a beautiful woman to open is her heart." He took a piece of chalk and marked Karen's bags as if he were putting the last touches on the Mona Lisa.

"Now, wasn't he a nice man?" Karen commented as we

7

all walked toward the taxis.

"Yeah," said William. "He was a real doll."

"They're all a bunch of bastards," Bartlett said, to himself more than anyone else.

## 2

WE WENT straight to the Hotel Excelsior. In the taxi Bartlett told William he was calling Stanton immediately. William agreed that this was a good idea. "It's against the American Constitution to send you to Sicily," William said.

Karen said as soon as she got to the hotel she was going to check the trains leaving for Rome in the morning.

I went upstairs to my room and unpacked. Then I opened the window and looked out at the harbor. I heard the noise of the streets, the screaming of the children, the bedlam that was and would probably always be Naples. I had made it. For a while it had looked as if I wouldn't. But good luck and the Internal Revenue Department were on my side.

It was a month ago, but it seemed as I looked down from my hotel room that it was at least a year.

It all started one day when I was sitting at the typewriter in the office and had just finished what I thought was a tre-

9

mendous lead for an article I was writing on juvenile delinquency.

"But aren't we all criminals?" I wrote.

"Pete," I said to myself as I stared at the line, "you may not have much talent, but you certainly can't write."

The telephone buzzed on my desk. I picked it up and heard the nervous voice of Mr. Matthew Lucas' secretary say, "Mr. Lucas would like to see you when you aren't busy."

When I wasn't busy? If I didn't get up to his office in three minutes I would be thrown out the twenty-fourth-floor window.

I grabbed my coat, straightened my tie, and tried to remember what I had put on my last expense account that I would be asked to justify.

Mr. Matthew Lucas was the publisher of the *News-Press*, but the only time you were called to his office was when he wanted to discuss a fiscal matter. He had more reasons why you couldn't get a raise than any other publisher in the United States. He could never understand why a reporter had to take a taxi when the "subway was so much quicker."

I was the chief crime reporter on the paper, but Mr. Lucas was hard put to accept the reasons why I had to take a policeman and/or a criminal to lunch. "The police are public servants," he would always say, "and the crooks can certainly pay for their own meals." It was a sore point in our relationship; at least it always got me sore.

I made it to his office in two minutes and twenty-nine

seconds, which was pretty good time considering I had to wait for the elevator.

Mr. Lucas' secretary greeted me with a sick smile and told me to go in.

My heart sank when I entered the room. Besides Lucas, who was sitting behind his large oak desk, I saw Harry Simpson, the managing editor, sitting on the couch, Walt King, the news editor, and Wilson Boyle, the syndicate manager, sitting in chairs. It looked like the *Caine Mutiny Court-Martial*.

Lucas nodded to me and told me to sit down.

"Pete," said Lucas, "we've been talking about you."

"I was afraid of that," was all I could say.

Simpson laughed. "Don't get upset, Pete, you haven't done anything wrong."

Lucas continued, "I understand you can speak Italian."

"I speak pretty good Italian," I acknowledged. I wasn't lying. We never spoke anything but Italian at home.

"Ever been to Italy?"

"Yeah," I replied, "during the war. I was with *Stars and Stripes* and I covered the Italian front."

"Do you have any desire to go back?"

"Are you thinking of opening an Italian bureau?"

"No, it's nothing like that," Simpson said. "We have a special assignment for you. It would require that you go to Italy for a month or so. How does that sound to you?"

"On full expenses?" I inquired.

Mr. Lucas looked peeved. "Don't you even want to know what the assignment is?"

Before I could answer Simpson said, "Pete, you've been

*11*

covering Frank Bartlett, so you know he's getting deported to Italy in a couple of weeks. We think it might be a good idea if you took the trip with him and wrote a series on what happens to a man like Bartlett when he gets deported. Boyle thinks he can sell the series through the syndicate."

"That, frankly," said Mr. Lucas, "is the only reason we can afford to let you go. If Boyle sells it we'll be off the hook for your expenses, which, incidentally, you'll have to watch."

"I knew there was a catch in it," I said. "You want me to go steerage?"

"Always the wise guy," said Walt King, the newspaper's leading apple wiper.

I was getting mad. "Look, Mr. Lucas," I said, "I'll go to Italy but I'm not going tourist class to save the paper money. If Bartlett goes first class, I'm going first class."

Simpson stepped in. "Of course, Pete. If Bartlett goes first class, you go first class."

I saw Mr. Lucas wince. I guess the thought of my having a cabin all to myself was too much for him.

Simpson stood up. "Okay, then, it's agreed. Pete goes on the S.S. *Continentale* with Bartlett."

"Don't forget," said Lucas to Simpson, "this was your idea, so it better be a good series."

"Bartlett has an appeal coming up, doesn't he?" Boyle said.

"Yes," I replied, "but it won't come up in the Supreme Court for a month. He's been trying to get a stay order, but he hasn't succeeded so he'll probably be out of the

12

country when the appeal is made."

"It's just as well," said Boyle. "As long as he stays in the newspapers it will help our cause."

"What are you working on now?" Lucas asked.

"Juvenile delinquency," I said. "I'm trying to prove juvenile delinquents would be just like other kids if you took away their switch blades and zip guns and hand-cuffed them to a psychiatrist every time they left the house."

Lucas didn't get the joke. "Let Sam Goodman write it. You'd better start researching Bartlett. We want this to be one helluva series, something none of the other papers will have. Go to it, Pete. We think a lot of you around here and we know you won't let us down."

"If the accounting department doesn't let me down, I won't let you down," I said.

As we left Lucas' office, King said, "You crime reporters always sound tougher than the people you write about."

"Go blow it, King," I said.

Simpson said, "Both of you knock it off."

I went off to the paper's morgue muttering to myself. Then suddenly I wanted to dance for joy. I had thought I was destined to spend the rest of my life running up and down the halls of the federal courthouse. I, who was willing to settle for a half-hour stroll on the boardwalk at Atlantic City, had suddenly been told I could go to Europe, first-class, on the *News-Press'* money. If Frank Bartlett had been there I would have kissed him. But then again, if Frank Bartlett had seen me looking so happy about his being deported, he might not have kissed me back.

*13*

I went down to the newspaper's morgue to do some research on the man. Word had already mysteriously spread through the paper about my trip, and when I walked into the morgue several people broke into "Arrivederci Roma."

Martha, the mountainous librarian, said, "Who says crime doesn't pay?"

"Martha," I said, "if you play your cards right, I'll put you in my suitcase."

Martha giggled. "You'll need a steamer trunk."

"Give me Frank Bartlett's folder. I have to do homework or they won't let me go."

Martha went to one of the big filing cabinets and pulled open a drawer. She hauled out three envelopes. "Which one do you want?" she asked.

"Let me have all of them." I replied.

If a man's fame in this world is based on how much has been written about him in the newspapers, then Frank Bartlett was indeed a famous man.

The three envelopes were full of clippings dating back to 1933, when Frank Bartlett was "discovered" as one of the youngest gambling operators on the East Coast.

I rifled through the clippings and suddenly came upon an article I had done on Frank Bartlett myself; a Sunday feature written five years ago. It was the first time I had met Frank Bartlett, although I had heard about him ever since I'd worked on the *News-Press*. Bartlett was to a crime reporter what Mickey Mantle was to a sports reporter. When the *News-Press* started to let you interview guys like Bartlett you knew you were on the way up.

*14*

The fact that I was of Italian descent didn't hurt me. Harry Simpson wasn't having any luck getting a man in to see Bartlett and he reasoned that I, being an Italian, might have a better chance of seeing him. He also figured I'd have more luck talking to Bartlett's old acquaintances in Italian. Simpson was right on both counts.

I called Bartlett and told him I was an East Side boy trying to make good on the *News-Press* and he reluctantly agreed to see me for a half hour in his apartment on Central Park West the following evening. I was so excited I couldn't sleep all night. I kept trying to memorize the questions I was going to ask him.

The next evening when I arrived at the apartment house I saw two hoods sitting in the lobby. I asked the elevator operator what floor Bartlett lived on and one of the hoods grunted that Bartlett was expecting me. The elevator operator took me up to the penthouse, which Bartlett apparently had all to himself.

The door was opened by a squat little man about five feet tall and almost as wide. He was wearing a white butler's jacket, but when he bowed I could see a .38 revolver sticking out of a holster under his arm. It was probably for dusting the furniture.

I waited in the living room a few minutes looking at all the brotherhood awards and golf and horse trophies that were on display. Then Bartlett came in. You think because a man is a big man in his work, he is probably a big man in size. But Bartlett was thin and only medium height. He was a good-looking fellow; a mixture of George Raft and Cary Grant. The fact that he was wearing a blue

15

velvet smoking jacket with a white scarf, gray flannel slacks and narrow pointed velvet slippers didn't hurt the Hollywood effect at all.

We shook hands and sat down on the couch.

The butler brought us drinks. It was the best Scotch I had ever tasted.

I started off by warning Bartlett that even though he had agreed to see me, the feature would not necessarily be complimentary.

"You're not telling me anything," he said. "Even if you want to write the truth your editors won't let you."

I said we'd print the truth if he'd level with me.

"Level with you? What do you want me to level with you? I'm a businessman. I own apartment houses, a laundry, a diaper service. You can go down to my accountant and look at my books. I've got nothing to hide."

"Why are people always taking pot shots at you?" I asked him.

"I don't know why," he said. "Probably because of the crap you guys write."

He pointed a cigar at me. "You guys cause all the trouble in the world. America would be a better place without newspapers."

"But how would people get the racing results?" I asked.

Bartlett calmed down. "Don't write what I just said. People will think I'm knocking America, which I'm not. I'm an American. Write that in the papers. I'm against all Commies and left-wing bastards. Say that."

I asked Bartlett about his family.

"That's my own personal business. Don't ask me any

questions about my family or about dames."

"Could you tell me in your own words why you never got married?"

"Why are you guys always digging into someone's personal life? That's an impertinent question."

"Mr. Bartlett," I said, taking a chance on ruining the interview, "you're a celebrity, just like Jack Benny, or Joe DiMaggio or General MacArthur. People want to know about you. What do you eat? Whom do you go out with, what do you think about? You owe it to the public."

"I don't owe the public anything," Bartlett said. "Anyway, I don't think publicity does you any good. Every time someone writes me up, I only have trouble with my businesses. As far as broads go, I like broads. Marriage is good for some guys, but I have to devote myself to my business. Wives are time-consuming. You see what I mean? Besides, as far as I'm concerned, William here can do anything a wife can do and better."

The butler smiled. "Not everything, boss."

"Yeah, except for that one thing," Bartlett agreed, "he can do everything."

We chatted about politics, the state of the nation, which Bartlett claimed he was concerned about, and horses. I felt as if I were sitting on a park bench with Bernard Baruch.

He gave me about forty-five minutes of his time, and while he evaded my leading questions I still managed to get a pretty good picture of him for my article.

As he showed me to the door he said, "You're probably going to dig up those old photographs of the movie

17

actresses again. I wish you'd use some new ones."

"If you're going out with a movie actress before next Sunday," I said, "would you call me. I'll send around my photographer."

He laughed and I thanked him for his time. Just as he opened the door a tall beautiful brunette arrived on the elevator and got off. I recognized her as a girl I had seen in the society pages of the *News-Press*; some debutante whose name I couldn't remember. Bartlett didn't introduce us, but he put his arm around her and said, "This is the only thing William can't do for me."

He chuckled and closed the door.

## 3

THE next day I went down to the lower East Side to talk to some of the people who had known Bartlett in his youth.

Someone directed me to a candy store, where I found an old man behind the soda fountain.

"Sure," he said, "I knew Frank Bartlett, only his name was Bartelini then. His father was a tailor, had a shop right down the street. Nice man. His mother was nice too. Everyone down here thinks Frank's a fine fellow. He gives milk to kids, turkeys on Thanksgiving and Christmas, and contributes to summer camps. Of course people thank Frank with votes for his candidates, but after all, one politician is just like another."

"You don't sound as if you like him."

"I don't like him or not like him. I just knew his father as a very fine man. He was poor but honest. Frank is rich and maybe he's not so honest. You won't get many people in this neighborhood to knock him, though; that is, until his body comes floating down the East River one of these days."

As we were talking a man walked into the store. "Here's my son Tony. He was Frank's best friend once. Tony, this fellow's a reporter. He's writing a story about Frank. My son Tony, he don't give no milk to kids, but I like it that way a lot better."

Tony looked about the same age as Bartlett, only he was much heavier. He was wearing a taxi driver's cap, a leather jacket and khaki pants. He went behind the counter and made himself a Coke.

When his father was out of earshot Tony said, "Don't mind Pop. He's from the old country. Frank's an okay guy. He just found an easier way to make a living than I did."

"Do you ever see him?"

"Nah. Once I was hacking up at the El Morocco and he got into my cab. But he was trying to make a dame and didn't recognize me. I got to be fair to Frank. When we were kids he offered to take me along with him all the way. I wanted to go into the Merchant Marine and see the world. Frank maintained the world was right here in Manhattan. You could go all around the earth, he said, but if you ever really wanted to make the big time, this was the place.

"This is probably a funny thing to say, but Frank was the most patriotic American I've ever known. He was always getting into arguments with guys who knocked the United States. He used to give his own parents hell because they didn't speak English at home. He even changed his name from Bartelini to Bartlett because it sounded more American. Frank said this was the only country that gave people a chance. He was a bug on the subject. He never finished public school, but I'll bet he knows more about American history than some college professors. I once kidded him about the fact that he could never become president of the United States because he wasn't born in the States, and he got sore and we had a fight."

Tony finished his Coke and washed his glass. "Frank might have made a good President, too, come to think of it."

I talked to a few other people, including two of Bartlett's sisters, a brother and a nephew. Only the brother, who worked as a watch repairman in a jewelry store, didn't think Bartlett was God's gift to New York.

The brother said, "Frank's values are all mixed up. He has to keep buying things with money . . . friends, girls, even his own family. But in his heart I think he is ashamed of us. I don't sit up and bark when he holds out a fifty-dollar bill, so he doesn't think much of me. But I feel sorry for him."

From others I discovered that Bartlett had been born in La Coma, Sicily, on January 14, 1914. He arrived in the United States when he was three years old. His father had opened a tailor shop on the lower East Side. Bartlett quit school when he was twelve years old and became a delivery boy for an East Side gang of bootleggers.

When he was around sixteen, he discovered a little thing called the floating crap game, but rather than compete in the games, he staged them, getting his share right off the top.

From then on it was a regular Horatio Alger story. He

21

branched out, first with pin-ball machines, then slot machines, and eventually bookie joints and numbers games. Not all his enterprises were crooked. Bartlett also bought real estate, laundry concessions, and politicians. By the time he was twenty-eight he had built up a multimillion-dollar empire.

He had moved uptown to his Central Park West apartment and tried to become respectable. He took up golf and sailing, and bought several horses. But he couldn't quite crack the country-club set, the yachting crowd or the Jockey Club. He kept getting blackballed every time his name came up for membership and apparently it played havoc with his ego.

At the same time he was rarely blackballed by a beautiful woman. One night-club owner I talked to once told me, "Bartlett may not be getting into their clubs, but he's sure getting into their daughters."

Naturally Bartlett's business associates wouldn't give me any dope on him, but the D.A. was a little more helpful.

He said, "Bartlett is one of the big wheels in the syndicate, a nation-wide gambling and racketeering organization. It's split up into territories and each group is supposed to stay within its boundaries. If someone covets another man's territory a protest is lodged with the syndicate by the injured party, and the syndicate decides what enforcement policies should be put in effect."

"It's just like the United Nations," I said.

"It works better than the United Nations. In fairness to Bartlett, though, we've never been able to trace any rough stuff to him. He's kind of a peacemaker. He knows there's a lot more money to be made if he stays out of the lime-light. But I'm sure if I could pin something on him the rest of his mob would fall apart at the seams."

It turned out that Bartlett had been arrested only three times, once for trying to bribe a basketball player, once for trying to bribe a judge and once for violating a city fire ordinance. He was never convicted of any of the charges.

Occasionally an ambitious non-member of the syndicate took a shot at him, but either aims were bad or Bartlett's bodyguards were too fast. In any case, he lived a charmed and what could be described as a rich life.

I put everything I had into the article, which I titled, "Flag-Waving Racketeer." Simpson was very pleased with the results, but when my mother read it she was sure she was going to lose her only son. Instead, when I came home from work the next day, I found a case of Bartlett's special Scotch waiting for me with an unsigned card, "I liked the article and you quoted me correctly."

I made the mistake of telling Simpson about the whisky and he said, "Send it back to the son-of-a-bitch."

It cost me two bucks to deliver it to his apartment.

The next day there were two cases, Bartlett probably thinking I wasn't satisfied with one. I took them back, which cost me another two bucks. It was becoming an expensive article for me.

In the morning, I received a call from William. "The boss says if you don't like to drink, you should go over and have a suit made by his tailor.

"It isn't that I don't like whisky," I told William, "but the paper won't let me accept the gift."

"Well, when the boss likes something, he wants to show it. So anything you want, let me know."

"Tell him all I want is that in the future I can see him when I call."

"I'll tell him that," said William. "Also, if your editor or anybody gives you trouble, let us know."

I saw Bartlett on and off for the next five years, usually in night clubs, where he was with either a movie actress or, more likely, a society girl.

Then I covered the famous Senate Crime hearings, which broke everybody up because Bartlett had a complete lapse of memory, and couldn't recall where he lived on the grounds that it would "incriminate" him. Somebody from the tax department must have been watching television that week, because before it was over the Internal Revenue Department made Bartlett "Man of the Year."

As it must with all racketeers investigated by the Internal Revenue Department, this attention eventually brought Bartlett to trial for cheating on taxes and out of this trial came the deportation proceedings.

I never wrote any more or any less about Bartlett's troubles during this period than the other reporters, but he had some idea I was on his side, and we got to see a lot of each other during recesses.

He called me "Pete" and left orders at all his night clubs that I wasn't to pick up a check. This didn't hurt my batting average with girls at all.

That Christmas he sent me a gold watch, one of those thin Patek Philippes, which was engraved on the inside,

24

"To Pete . . . a newspaperman I can trust. F.B."

I kept the watch, but this time I didn't tell Simpson.

When I found out I was going to accompany Bartlett to Europe I called him on the phone to break the happy news to him.

"Guess what, Mr. Bartlett. The newspaper is giving me a free trip to Europe."

"That's fine," he said. "Have a good time. I'll see you when you get back."

"But I'm going with you," I said. "They want me to follow you around and tell our readers what a good time you're having."

"Crap," said Bartlett angrily. "I'm not going. They can't make that deportation order stick. I've got my lawyers working on it now."

"That may be so, but I've been checking around and the Justice Department is determined you're going to get your boat ride. This is a big feather in their cap and they're not going to let anybody spoil it."

"But I'm an American citizen," Bartlett said. "They can't deport an American citizen. I left Italy when I was three years old.

"Well, for my records, just in case the stay order isn't granted in time, will that mean you're leaving on the *Continentale*?"

"They've got me reservations on the *Continentale*, but they're going to have a hard time putting me on the ship."

"They may throw you in the pen," I warned.

"They don't have the guts. Kid, I'll tell you what. If I don't go, I'll treat you to a boat ride without me. I don't want you cheated out of a trip."

I wanted to say it would be more fun if I could go with him, instead I said, "Thanks a lot. I might hold you to it."

The *Continentale* was scheduled to leave on Tuesday. Wetherby Stanton, Bartlett's top legal eye, was hopping between Albany, New York and Washington trying to find a friendly judge who would stop the proceedings. But Bartlett was a hot property. The newspapers had front-paged his deportation and as each day passed the bookies' odds that Bartlett would go were getting higher and higher. Not even Bartlett's highest connections, and they were pretty high, could do anything for him. I was sure I would see the Isle of Capri within a week.

On Monday, when it was obvious Bartlett would have to leave, I went in to see Simpson, who was grinning from ear to ear.

"I was afraid the son-of-a-bitch might beat the rap," he said. "We're going to give him a nice bon-voyage editorial."

"Harry," I said, "I don't care if Bartlett gets deported or not, but if you run one of your typical 'farewell to deportees' editorials, you're not going to make my job any easier."

"You have a point," Simpson said. "We'll save the editorial for after the series. Now, Pete, here's what we want from you. I don't know what happens to a man after he gets deported from the United States. Neither do our readers. "What we want is the whole story of what happens to a big shot when he goes back to his native land.

"Cable the arrival story as straight news and any other stories you think will make news. As for the series, take your time. We'll give you about a month. Stick with him no matter where he goes or what he does. When you think you've got the whole picture, let us know. You don't have to write the series there, but you'd better fly back so you won't waste any time.

"The cashier has your boat ticket, your plane ticket and a thousand dollars for expenses. You probably won't need as much as that."

"Not if I do without lunch and dinner," I said.

"Anyway, here's a credit card for the Italian post office so you can send your news stories collect."

I nodded and got up to leave.

"One more thing, Pete," Simpson said. "I argued against Lucas and King for you to go on this assignment. Make this a good series or they'll be out for your neck."

"Don't worry about my neck, Harry. It's been wrung before."

We shook hands.

Simpson looked down and said, "That's a nice watch you've got there."

I got red in the face. "My mother gave it to me as a going-away present."

Simpson looked at me. "You certainly have a nice mother."

"See you in a month," I said, heading for the door fast.

"Oh, Pete," Simpson said as I was shutting the door. I opened it and stood there. "Bon voyage."

"Thanks, Harry," I said. "I'll remember that."

# 4

THE S.S. *Continentale*, leaving for Gibraltar, Cannes, Genoa and Naples, was docked at West Forty-sixth Street. I was now on expenses, so I took a taxi. Besides, when you're going to Europe first class, it doesn't look very good if you arrive on a bus. Trucks and cabs were everywhere. People were being paged, policemen were blowing their lungs out and everyone seemed to be yelling at everyone else. I was glad I talked my mother out of seeing me off on the boat. She was a little upset about my going, and packed enough food to last me the trip. She didn't believe modern ocean liners fed their passengers. They hadn't on the ship she came over on.

I went through the passport and ticket formalities and was just going to proceed up the gangplank when I saw Bartlett pull up in a long Cadillac. To him it must have felt like riding in a hearse. He was with his lawyer, Wetherby Stanton.

A group of photographers and reporters who were wait-

28

ing by the gangplank rushed over to him.

"Hey, Mr. Bartlett," a photographer shouted. "How about a shot of you reading the deportation order?"

Bartlett, who was impeccably dressed in a charcoal-gray pin-striped suit, white shirt and black tie, scowled and tried to push his way through the crowd.

Stanton was shouting, "Mr. Bartlett has nothing to say."

Bartlett whispered something to Stanton and then held up his hand. "Okay, quiet down. I'll give you a statement."

The reporters had their pencils poised as the photographers kept snapping photos.

"As I said at my trial, I was framed by the Attorney General on income tax evasion. The Attorney General and I are political enemies and this is his way of getting back at me. Since the Justice Department won't let me wait for my appeal, I'm going to Europe for a month and will be back for the opening of Hialeah. I'm sure all Americans will agree with me that this deportation is not only unconstitutional but un-American."

"Will you look up Joe Adonis and Lucky Luciano when you get to Italy, Mr. Bartlett?"

"I'm sorry, but I don't know either one of those gentlemen. I have no plans to see anyone. I'm on vacation."

"Will you visit the town in Sicily where you were born?"

"I don't expect to go to Sicily. I plan to visit London, Paris, the Riviera, Rome and Capri."

"Suppose your appeal is denied. Where will you settle in Italy?"

"My appeal won't be denied. I'm an American. I have my rights."

"But you had the choice of going to Italy or an American penitentiary. If you're an American, why didn't you go to the pen?'"

While the question was being asked, I saw Stanton signal to some stevedores, who came over and started to shove the reporters back.

They made a hole for Bartlett and Stanton to get through. The reporters tried to follow, but the stevedores made menacing gestures with their fists.

"Hey, what do you think you guys are doing?" a reporter shouted. One of the stevedores smashed a photographer's camera.

"Mr. Bartlett don't want his picture took," the stevedore said. The reporters retreated slowly. I ducked around, flashed my boarding pass and was on deck waiting for Bartlett when he came up.

When Bartlett stepped on deck, I said, "Hi, Mr. Bartlett. I made it."

Bartlett, who was probably still sore at the newspapermen, scowled at me. "Well, it's going to be a dull trip and your newspaper is wasting its money."

"But I need the rest," I protested.

Barlett laughed and punched me on the shoulder.

"Frank," said Stanton, "your stateroom is this way."

Since no one had told me not to, I tagged along with them.

"That was some reception committee you had down below," I said.

"You mean those reporters?" Bartlett said.

"No, the stevedores."

"Ah," he replied. "They're just friends of Tony Agnello. They didn't want anyone to get hurt."

Just before we reached Bartlett's stateroom suite Stanton said, "I'm sorry as hell about this Frank. . . . I . . . I . . ."

"Stop blubbering," Bartlett snapped. "Just don't goof on the appeal."

"You can count on me, Frank," Stanton said. "The Justice Department is going to be sorry they ever heard of Frank Bartlett. . . . here's your suite."

Stanton opened the door.

When I looked in I saw the stateroom jammed with men. Bartlett seemed as surprised as I was.

He turned to Stanton. "What's going on?"

Stanton said, "A little surprise the boys cooked up."

Someone spotted Bartlett and yelled. All of a sudden they broke into "For He's a Jolly Good Fellow." They grabbed Bartlett and pulled him into the stateroom. I squeezed into the suite before they shut the door. Someone shoved a drink into my hand. Bartlett was also handed a drink. Then Tommy Thompson, whom I knew as one of Bartlett's lieutenants, stood on a chair and shouted for silence.

The room quieted down. "Frank," he said, "the boys all want you to know although you got a raw deal, we know you'll be back with us again in a month and we hope you consider this as we do, a vacation you so richly deserve."

"That's right," someone said.

"As a token of our esteem and to remind you of us in your travels no matter where you go, we have chipped in together and bought you . . . we assure you, Frank, they are not hot goods . . . a few things. First," he said, holding up a package, "is a Polaroid camera which takes pictures and develops them in thirty seconds. No tourist should be without one."

There was lots of laughing as he handed Bartlett the package. He held up another. "This is a transistor radio. It doesn't need batteries and it's no bigger than a gun. William can wear it in his shoulder holster."

More laughter.

"There's one more thing, but you'll be hearing about it later. Frank, there is no more that I can say. There isn't a man in this room who doesn't owe you a debt of gratitude. You put our organization on the map and we'll never forget that. We wish you bon voyage."

Bartlett stood on the chair and as the applause subsided he said, "Thanks for the going-away party. I appreciate the send-off and these gifts. I only wish you were going away instead of me."

There was slight embarrassed laughter.

"But I know," continued Bartlett, "while I'm gone the organization will run just as smoothly as if I were here. . . . It's taken a long time to build up the business and we must look forward to continued prosperity. Anyone who makes any mistakes or gets out of line is going to have to answer personally to me."

The loud-speaker announced that visitors had to leave.

"That's all. Let's make this a banner year."

"And let's bankrupt Rizzolli," someone shouted.

Everyone cheered.

Steve Rizzolli, I knew, was the head of a rival syndicate

from New Jersey that had recently been giving Bartlett a bad time.

They started shaking hands with Bartlett and leaving.

Red Munzelli, another of Bartlett's lieutenants, was one of the last to leave. He gave Bartlett a package.

"It's all there, Frank. Seventy-five G's in cash. My brother, he used to be a tourist, said you can get a better rate for the dollar if you have cash."

"Thanks," said Bartlett. "I'll give it to William for safe-keeping. Keep in touch, Red."

Stanton was the last to go. "I'll cable you as soon as the appeal is made, Frank. You've got nothing to worry about. It's in the bag."

Bartlett, William and I were the only people left in the stateroom. He was surprised to see I was still there. "What are you doing here?"

"No one gave me a going-away party, so I thought I'd stay for yours."

"Yeah, well anything you heard here just now is off the record, you understand? As a matter of fact, if you're going to be in my hair on this trip, I'm going to lay down the rules. When I say something is off the record, it's off the record. You got that?"

"Sure," I said, "I'll play by the rules."

"Okay," Bartlett said. He took off his neatly pressed suit coat and gave it to William. "I'm going to take a bath."

"Wait a minute, boss, you don't want to take a bath yet."

"What do you mean, I don't want to take a bath yet?"

William looked upset. "For one thing, the guys from Immigration are still outside." William opened the door. "You see?"

Bartlett looked at the Immigration men. "I thought you guys had left."

"We're going out as far as the pilot boat, Mr. Bartlett," one of them said.

"Well, come in and have a glass of champagne."

"I'll have a beer if you've got one," one of the men offered.

"Me too," his partner said.

"William, two beers for the gentlemen, a Scotch for my reporter friend and the same for me. And open up a can of caviar."

William served the drinks and Bartlett and the Immigration men raised their glasses. "Good trip, Mr. Bartlett," one of the men said.

"Thanks, gentlemen. You've been pretty discreet and I'm going to put in a good word for you when I get back to Washington."

"That's very generous of you, Mr. Bartlett. Very generous indeed."

"Hey, look, Mr. Bartlett," I said as I stared out the porthole. "There's the Statue of Liberty."

Bartlett walked over to where I was standing and looked out the porthole. He raised his glass. "So long, sister, I'll be seeing you sooner than you think."

William laughed and opened the can of caviar.

In an hour Bartlett and I were pretty tanked up. The Immigration men had gone and we were already planning what we were going to do when we hit Paris. I told Bartlett I heard that the streets were paved with mattresses. He said he knew of a rich society dame who had her yacht in Venice and it was more than likely we would be invited on board.

William didn't seem to be enjoying himself.

Bartlett said to him, "William, relax, relax."

William turned and looked at both of us. "Boss," he said, "can he be trusted?"

Bartlett laughed. "Sure, William. Pete's like a brother to me."

"You can say that again," I agreed.

"Okay," William said, "because I got something to show you."

"Let's have a drink before you go showing me things," Bartlett said.

"No surprises without drinks," I concurred.

William reluctantly made some drinks.

Then he said, "The boys . . . that is, all the fellows in the organization, were racking their brains for weeks trying to think of something to get you."

"They gave me a camera and a radio."

"No," said William, "that's just chicken feed. They wanted to get you something real nice, something that would make your trip more pleasant. I'm not saying I was for or against the idea . . . either way I was overruled."

"For God's sake," said Bartlett, "get to the point."

"Okay," William said. He went over to the door, looked at us and then opened it. A beautiful blonde girl . . . at first I thought it was Ginger Rogers, but a young Ginger

Rogers . . . was sitting on the bed in a mink coat. She looked terribly nervous and uncomfortable.

"We've struck oil," I shouted.

Bartlett pushed me down.

William looked at her and said, "But you're not the one. The other one was a redhead!"

"Shirley couldn't come," the blonde said and I thought she was going to cry.

By this time Bartlett had sobered up and he shouted, "What's that broad doing in my suite?"

William said to the blonde, "Come out here."

She hesitated and then walked into the sitting room. She had a beautiful figure, with nice long legs and a lovely face, even if it was encased in fear.

William said, "Boss, I want you to meet your gift from the boys."

"My what?"

"It's your going-away gift from the boys. This is Miss . . . Miss . . . Miss . . ."

The blonde bit her lip. "Miss Karen Withers."

"Yeah," said William, "that's her name and she's from the road company of *My Fair Lady*."

"Has everyone gone out of his mind? What the hell do I want with a broad?"

William smiled. "That's a funny question for you to ask, boss. What does any guy want with a broad?"

"That isn't what was agreed upon," Karen said.

"Shut up," William replied.

Bartlett was shouting at William, "If I wanted a broad to come along with me, I would have brought one."

36

"The fellows figured you were so busy you might have forgot."

"Judas Priest," said Bartlett. "Am I going nuts?"

"My feet hurt," said Karen. "Can I sit down?"

"Not in my suite, sister," Bartlett said. "You'd better get off the boat."

"It's too late," William pleaded. "The boys were afraid you'd react like this, so they made me promise I wouldn't give her to you until we got outside the three-mile limit. They went to an awful lot of trouble to get her. They bought her a ticket and outfitted her from head to toe. It cost them a lot of dough. You have no idea the price of women's clothes these days. The boys would be crushed if you didn't take her. There might even be a morale problem."

"I have an idea," I said. "Why don't you give her to me?"

Bartlett wheeled on me. "You keep out of this. And this is off the record too."

"I'm sorry, Mr. Bartlett. But it's not a bad gift."

"Nobody gives me dames," he said, and went into his own bedroom and slammed the door.

William turned to Karen. "Now, what's the story? How come you're here instead of Shirley?"

Karen said, "Shirley was sick. She had to have an operation. I'm her roommate and she suggested I go in her place. But she explained it a lot differently." Tears were coming to her eyes.

"Didn't Shirley tell you who you'd be traveling with?"

"She said a Mr. Bartlett. But I didn't know it was *this*

Mr. Bartlett. Shirley said he was sick and eighty years old and was afraid to travel alone. I've seen this Bartlett on television. If I'd known this I would never have come."

Karen was sniffling. "I've never done anything like this before. My mother would die if she knew I was traveling with a gangster."

"Don't start crying," William said. "Apparently from what the boss said, you ain't going to be seeing much of him anyway. But since you signed up for this trip, you're going to have to be real nice to him, no matter if he's nice to you or not. I promised the boys I'd see that the boss had a good time. It may take a few days for him to loosen up, but in the meantime you have to do what I tell you."

"It all depends," Karen said defiantly, "what you tell me to do."

"Be a good girl," said William, patting her on the hand. "The boss has been through a lot during the past year. We've both got to make him forget."

"Both of us?"

"Yeah," said William angrily. "Both of us, and especially you."

# 5

THAT night I met Bartlett and William in the bar before dinner.

William was trying to persuade Bartlett to dine in the main dining room.

"A lot of people will bother me," Bartlett objected.

"Who's going to bother you?" William protested. "We're just tourists like anybody else. Nobody knows who you are. I arranged a table on the side so you wouldn't attract attention."

After a couple of drinks we went down to the main dining room, where Archie, the headwaiter, showed us to a table.

Bartlett asked Archie for a menu, and, after ordering, returned it with a fifty-dollar bill attached.

"That's so nobody bothers me," Bartlett said.

"I understand perfectly," Archie said, bowing so deeply I thought his chin was going to hit the table. "Leave everything to me."

The waiter had just served the soup when we noticed a stir in the dining room. I looked up and saw Karen standing in the door. She was wearing a gold lamé evening dress and a diamond tiara which looked almost real.

Everyone was staring.

"Oh, my God," Bartlett said.

William said, "Jeeze, we forgot all about her."

Archie rushed over and bowed. But when Karen spoke to him, he seemed confused. He looked at her again, shrugged his shoulders and escorted her to our table.

I was the only one who bothered to get up.

Archie said helplessly, "She says she's in your party."

William nodded. "More or less."

People in the dining room were grinning.

We heard the woman at the next table say, "I'm sure it's him. The morning paper said he was being deported."

A man at the table said, "With a girl like that it couldn't be anybody else."

Another woman at the table said, "George, why don't you get his autograph for little Jerry? He'd be thrilled."

A fourth man said, "I wouldn't, George. He may be carrying a gun. His pocket seems to be bulging."

Karen said, "I thought everyone was supposed to dress for dinner on an ocean liner."

"Not on the first night," I said.

"Well, nobody told me anything about it. As a matter of fact, nobody's told me about anything. What am I supposed to do?"

"Keep quiet, for one thing," Bartlett said.

"If you don't mind my saying it, Mr. Bartlett," Karen said, "you don't seem to be having a very good time."

"I do mind your saying it," Bartlett said. "I'm not asking anything of you except to leave me alone."

"All right," Karen said, "but I'm not going to eat alone. I've never been on a ship before and I'm going to have a good time."

She studied the menu. "Is it true you can have all the caviar you want?" she asked Archie.

Archie bowed. "As much as you wish."

"Isn't that wonderful?" Karen asked us excitedly.

"What would you like to drink?"

"Champagne. I want champagne."

"If you'll permit me," Archie said, "vodka goes better with caviar."

"All right," said Karen, "I'll have vodka now and champagne later."

The waiter brought the can of caviar, which was set in a carved statue of ice, representing, I think, the Venus de Milo. The wine steward poured out a glass of vodka.

"Well, cheers," Karen said.

"Cheers," I replied.

Karen sipped the vodka and coughed.

She gasped, "It didn't *look* so strong!"

She started eating her caviar.

"Who wants to go to the movies after dinner?" she said. "It's a new film that's never been shown on land."

Bartlett said, "I have work to do."

"Me too," William said.

"I might go with you," I said.

Karen suddenly looked up at me. "Who are you anyway?"

"I'm just a newspaperman taking a trip to Europe."

*41*

"That's funny," said Karen, after drinking the rest of her vodka. "I thought you were his bodyguard. You look like a bodyguard."

"It must be the way my pad and pencil stick out of my coat pocket."

The waiter had refilled Karen's glass and she knocked the vodka down like a pro. "It's not bad once you get used to it."

William said, "Be careful. It will hit you over the head."

A minute or two passed and nobody said anything. Then Karen, who was on her third vodka, turned to Bartlett. "Mr. Bartlett, may I ask you one question?"

"Yes," said Bartlett wearily.

"Are you a white slaver?"

Bartlett almost spilled his soup on his pants.

"What?"

"Are you a white slaver? Do you kidnap girls and sell them for prostitution?"

Bartlett got himself composed.

"No, Miss Withers, I'm not a white slaver. Why do you ask?"

"Because when I saw you on television you refused to answer on the grounds it would incriminate you."

"I refused to answer any questions on television."

"Well, you know, when I was watching the hearings, I said to myself, 'He's probably not a white slaver.' I've got intuition about those things."

"Thank you very much," Bartlett said, starting to eat his soup again.

"What about dope?"

Bartlett choked. "I never take it."

"Or sell it?"

"Never."

William became indignant. "You should be ashamed of yourself. The boss is a respectable businessman, and girls and dope are the lowest things you can say about a guy."

"Don't get all excited," Karen said. "A party has a right to know who she's traveling with."

"The boss was never mixed up in dope and girls. You can ask J. Edgar Hoover if you don't believe me. Do you know what rap the boss is trying to beat?"

"I don't have any idea," Karen said.

"Income taxes. Do you know how many people cheat on income taxes? One hundred and ninety million people in the United States alone."

"But why didn't he pay?" Karen asked.

"It wasn't a question of not paying," William said. "The boss forgot to send in returns for a couple of years. It could have happened to you."

Karen shook her head. "Not me. They take my income taxes out before they give me my salary. It's called withholding."

"What about those clothes you're wearing?" said William. "And the ticket that was bought for you? That's income."

"You have to do something for income," Karen said. "And I'm not doing anything."

"You can say that again," Bartlett muttered.

The man named George at the next table leaned over with his menu and said, "Mr. Bartlett, can I have your autograph for my nephew?"

William pushed the menu back. "Screw, mister."

George became red in the face and turned to the people at his table. "No wonder they're deporting him. It's about time America got rid of all of them."

"Hush, George," his wife cautioned. "The gun."

"Come on," Bartlett said to William. "Let's get out of here."

He got up. William followed him. Everyone watched as they left the dining room.

One of the women at George's table said in a loud whisper, "The blonde must be his moll."

Karen, who was on her fourth vodka, looked at me. "Do you hear what they're saying? Oh dear, what am I going to do?"

"Miss Withers . . ."

"Call me Karen, it's easier for both of us. What's your name?"

"Pete. Pete Angelino. Look, Karen, this is off the record, but I'm kind of curious. How did you wind up on this trip?"

Karen looked sadly at the caviar. "It was all Shirley's fault," she replied. "She wasn't sick as I said. She had agreed to go. She told me she was going with a sick man eighty years old who liked to have young pretty girls around him. It sounded so innocent.

"She kept buying all these fancy clothes and tiaras and I thought she had hit an oil well or something. But the day before yesterday, her boy friend found out about it and he raised the roof. She has some strange boy friends,

44

but this one is really crazy and said if she went he would do all sorts of things to her. Shirley cried and said she had to go, but he became more violent. Finally she said she wouldn't. Then she started working on me. She said I had to go to save her life.

"I really want to be a movie star and everyone told me if I went to Rome I'd have a chance to get into the movies because they don't have many girls there who speak English. I have a friend who knows the casting director of *Ben Hur* and she said if I could get to Rome she'd get me a job in the picture. Shirley said this would be the easiest way to get in the movies.

"Well, I'm her size, and all her clothes fit me, and everything happened so fast that she talked me into it. But I swear I didn't know what I was getting into. Now I may not even get to Rome. He may kill me right on the boat."

"No," I said, "Bartlett isn't that kind. Frankly, I think you're pretty safe. Bartlett is a pretty conceited guy and he likes to pick his own girls. His ego was hurt because the boys in his mob had to get him a girl. He probably won't even lay a hand on you."

"What about that thug, William?"

"He's harmless. He does anything Bartlett tells him."

"Well," said Karen, "I'm glad you're along. At least there will be a witness if anything happens to me."

"Nothing will happen to you. You'll probably get off the boat and go straight to Rome."

Karen put her hand on mine. "You're very nice. I hope we can be friends."

45

I put my hand on hers, but she pulled it away. "I said friends. I don't want any trouble from you. I've got enough as it is."

For a guy on his first ocean voyage, I was batting zero.

"Come on, let's go to the movie," I said.

"Gee," she said, cheering up, "it's fun to see movies before they get to Radio City Music Hall."

"That," I said, "is why most people take a boat."

# 6

THE next morning I found Bartlett and William on the sun deck resting in deck chairs. Bartlett was wearing a blue blazer, gray flannels and a yachtsman's cap. I felt out of place in my tweed suit.

He looked up when I arrived and said, "How are you doing with my gift?"

"I took her to the movies, but either the vodka or the caviar was too much for her. Besides, I don't think they should show pictures about submarines aboard an ocean liner."

Bartlett laughed.

William was scowling and muttering.

"What's wrong with you?" I asked.

"We interviewed twenty dames before we found the right one. This redheaded Shirley was just perfect. She spoke our language. The guys gave her a blank check to buy anything she wanted. They were like kids. So what happens? She double-crosses us and sends this bird-brain instead. You can't trust dames."

"She's a nice kid," I said.

"Who needs a nice kid on a trip like this?" William asked. "What we wanted for the boss was a dame."

"Well, let this be a lesson to you, William," Bartlett said. "I'll pick my own dames from now on. We'll dump her in Naples."

"Sure, boss," said William. "Anything you say. I wanted everything to be so right for you this trip. You deserve it."

"You've got to admit, Pete, William is a loyal man."

I took the empty deck chair next to Bartlett's and sat down. Bartlett started to read the *Wall Street Journal*.

"Are you a heavy investor in stocks?" I asked.

"Nah," said Bartlett. "I don't trust those monkeys. They don't know how to run a business. You give your dough to a guy you never heard of and he can do anything he wants with it. I just like to read the *Journal* to see what's up. It's like a baseball game to me."

I was reading *Time* magazine. In a few minutes the deck steward came over with a card and said, "Excuse me, Signore, would you care to enter the ship's pool?"

"What's the pitch?" Bartlett said.

"You select a number from one to ten," the steward said, "and you pay five dollars. The ship travels a certain number of miles per day. Every day the mileage is posted at noon on the passenger bulletin board. If the ship does four hundred fifty-six miles and you are holding the number six, then you win. It's the last digit that counts."

"How much can you win?" Bartlett asked.

"Forty-five dollars," the steward replied.

"The ship's cut is ten per cent, huh?"

"Yes," said the steward. "It's for sailors' welfare."

"Okay, I'll take one. Give me number three. Maybe my luck will change."

The steward wrote out Bartlett's name next to number three. Bartlett gave him five dollars.

"What about you, Signore?" he asked me.

I shook my head. "Maybe tomorrow."

Five minutes later William got up, stretched and said, "I guess I'll take a walk around the deck." He wandered off without either of us saying anything.

I fell asleep and must have been dozing for about forty minutes when I heard voices.

I awoke to see a ship's officer and two sailors standing over our chairs.

The officer said, "Signore Bartlett, the Captain would like to see you."

Bartlett was annoyed. "If he wants to see me, let him come here."

"No," said the officer, "when the Captain wants to see you, you have to go to him. That is why he is called the Captain."

"I'm not moving out of this chair."

The people in the other deck chairs were following the scene with interest.

The officer told the sailors to stay by the chairs and he went off down the sun deck toward the bridge.

"What's up?" I said.

"Beats the hell out of me. But you would think with the prices they charge you on this ferry boat, they'd leave you alone."

49

In a few moments, the Captain, a short, rotund, red-faced, excitable Italian, came charging down the deck, with an officer at his heels.

Everyone was sitting up in his deck chair now.

"Signor Bartlett?" he said after the officer had pointed him out.

"Yeah, what do you want?"

"I run a pleasure ship. I don't interfere with the passengers on this ship unless they interfere with me."

"Who's interfering with your ship?"

"You may think bribing an officer of my ship is a joke, but I assure you it's not a laughing matter."

"What are you talking about?"

"You know what I'm talking about." He handed Bartlett a slip of paper. I read it over his shoulder. It was printed and it said, "IF YOU CAN MAKE THE MILEAGE FOR THE DAY END IN NUMBER THREE THERE IS TWENTY BUCKS IN IT FOR YOU."

"The officer of the deck was handed this note no more than twenty minutes ago," the Captain said. "What number do you hold in the pool?"

"Three," said Bartlett. "But I had nothing to do with this note."

"Ha," the Captain snorted. "I know all about you, Signor Bartlett. You may be a big gambler in the United States, but nobody fixes the pools on my ship."

"Get out of here, you tin-horn sailor," Bartlett shouted angrily, "or I'll really lose my temper."

"Tin-horn sailor, am I?" screamed the Captain. "I'll show you who's a tin-horn sailor. You're confined to your cabin for the rest of the trip. Get down there now!"

"You can't do this to me. I'm a paying passenger," Bartlett screamed back.

"Don't tell me what I can do on my ship. Do you want my men to carry you down to your cabin, or would you prefer the brig?"

"Who told you I fixed the pool? Who?"

The Captain made a gesture toward the sailors, who picked up Bartlett and began dragging him down the deck.

Bartlett shouted, "I'll sue you." He screamed, "I'll sue you for a million dollars."

The Captain turned to the rest of the people in the deck chairs and bowed. "Please, I'm sorry I lost my temper. But no one has ever tried to fix the ship's pool before."

"We'll back you, Captain, in case you have any trouble with the company," a man in one of the chairs said. "We Americans aren't very proud of him."

"Thank you." The Captain bowed again and walked away.

The whole thing bothered me. It didn't sound like Bartlett. Why would he want to fix the pool for forty-five dollars? Yet he was holding number three. Then suddenly it hit me. I wondered how long it would take to hit Bartlett.

In the afternoon I went down to Bartlett's cabin. William was pressing one of Bartlett's suits. He looked pretty sick.

"Where is he?" I said.

"He's in there," William said, indicating the closed bedroom door. "He just killed a bottle of Scotch."

"That was quite a stroll you took this morning," I said.

William looked up, frightened. "Sh . . . sh . . . sh . . ."

"I was sure it had to be you. No one else would have written that note."

"I was only trying to make the boss happy," William said, whimpering. "I figured if he won the pool he would think his luck was changing. I didn't know they'd get so mad."

"They got mad all right," I said. "I thought they were going to throw Bartlett to the sharks."

William shook his head. "Why doesn't anything I do ever come out right?"

"Does he know?"

"No," said William. "He thinks Rizzolli framed him. He got drunk and cabled the boys to wreck Rizzolli's warehouse. I couldn't stop it without him finding out I did it. You won't tell him I did it?" William pleaded.

"I might and I might not," I said. "It all depends on you."

"What do you mean?"

"I've got to do this series and it's got to be good. All I want you to do is fill me in on details of things that happen when I'm not around."

"That's blackmail," William said.

"It's better than Bartlett finding out who wrote that note."

"Okay," said William, "but don't say anything to him. Promise?"

"You can count on me," I told William. "Where's Karen?"

"I don't know."

I found Karen up in the lounge talking to a natty little man in a checkered suit.

Karen introduced me as her press agent. "And this, Pete, is Mr. Riccardo Fiorentino, the very well-known Italian producer." She hit the "well-known" hard. I had never heard of him and I was sure Karen hadn't either.

I gulped and shook hands.

"I was telling your client," Fiorentino said, "that she is perfect for the girl I am looking for in my new film, *South of Naples.* She could be another Gina Lollobrigida."

"Or Sophia Loren," I suggested.

"Do you know what I want to do with you?" the producer said, taking Karen's hand.

"What?" asked Karen breathlessly.

"I want to make a co-production."

Fiorentino was practically panting. "Yes, an Italian-American co-production starring Karen Withers and produced by Riccardo Fiorentino and Frank Bartlett."

"Oh," said Karen, withdrawing her hand. "So that's it. I better warn you, Mr. Bartlett isn't going to produce anything I play in."

"But," protested Fiorentino, "you are his woman."

"Only until I get to Rome."

"And he wouldn't put up any money to aid your career?"

"Not in a million years."

Fiorentino got up and kissed Karen's hand. "Perhaps you should appear in *Ben Hur* first." He departed hurriedly.

Karen sighed. "Getting into the movies is much harder than I thought it would be."

The following days I spent dividing my time between Bartlett and Karen. Bartlett was in a vile mood and William told me that after he had ordered the gang to set fire to one of Rizzolli's warehouses, Rizzolli had retaliated and wrecked fourteen of Bartlett's laundry trucks. There was probably a whole section in the Bronx where people were walking around in dirty shirts. I hated to think what would happen if the diaper service broke down. But the fact that Rizzolli took revenge made Bartlett more positive that Rizzolli had framed him on the ship. If he had thought it out clearly, he would have realized that Rizzolli couldn't possibly have known what number Bartlett took in the pool. But Bartlett was so obsessed with anger and liquor that he wasn't thinking too clearly.

Karen, on the other hand, was having the time of her life. I kept her company as much as I could, and I was pitching at her all the time. But she would never take me seriously. She kept pointing out other women on the ship that she believed I could have better luck with. It was frustrating but at the same time I really was beginning to fall for her.

I guess I realized how far overboard I had gone a few nights before we were scheduled to dock at Naples.

I was playing three-handed gin rummy with Bartlett and William in their sitting room when he suddenly picked up the cards and threw them against the wall. "I'm going out of my bloody mind," he said. "This is worse than being in the stir."

William said, "I don't blame you, boss. Of course, outside of playing cards you might look in on our blonde friend in the next room. At least it would relieve the monotony."

My heart sank as I looked at Bartlett.

He stood up. "William, sometimes you have some pretty good ideas."

Bartlett went to his own bedroom, shaved, put some toilet water on himself, and came out in a maroon dressing gown.

"What am I going to do?" I said to myself. "I may have to poke him and that will be the end of the series and even the end of me. Steady, boy, steady."

Bartlett went over to Karen's door and knocked softly on it. There was no reply. He knocked harder.

"Who is it?" I heard Karen say.

"It's me," Bartlett replied sweetly.

"What do you want?" Karen asked.

"I want to speak to you."

"Speak to me tomorrow."

Bartlett banged on the door some more. "You open up!"

"Are you trying to get in bed with me?" Karen said.

Bartlett was angry. "Well, what if I am? What the hell did you think you came along on the trip for?"

Karen yelled, "Nobody said anything about sleeping with you."

William looked at me in amazement. "Have you ever heard anything like that in your life?"

Bartlett was now banging on the door furiously. He said, "Open up! Do you hear me?"

Karen yelled out, "Not on your life, Buster."

William ran over to the door and started pounding.

"Karen, this is William. Please open the door. The boss is real lonely."

She yelled back, "Tell him to take a cold shower."

I could have kissed her.

I thought Bartlett was going to break the door down, but instead he turned around and walked toward his own room. "I never begged a dame for it before," he said, "and I'm not going to start now."

William came back to the table boiling. "I'd like to shove her teeth down her throat. Can you imagine her turning down the boss' favors after all the boys did for her?"

I was so happy I wanted to shout, but instead I said, "There are a lot of ungrateful people in this world, William. But you have to go on a trip with them before you find out who they are."

"Yeah," said William, "I guess you're right."

The next morning I met Karen on deck. She looked more beautiful than ever in a dark blue cashmere sweater and blue slacks.

I didn't mention what had happened on the previous night, as I wasn't sure whether she had known if I was there or not, but William came storming on deck and told her, "That wasn't a nice thing you did last night to the boss. The boys are going to be pretty sore."

"I can't stand people being rude to me," she said.

"If it makes the boss happy to be rude to you, then you have to let him be rude to you. No one forced you to come on this trip. You came of your own free will."

Tears were starting to come to Karen's eyes.

"Aw, William," I said, "lay off. The girl is confused."

"Not half as confused as I am," he said.

"Come on, Karen," I said, "I'll play some deck tennis with you."

"Sure, go ahead," said William. "Have a good time while the boss sits it out in his room down below."

"William," I said, "whose fault is it if Bartlett is stuck in his cabin?"

William muttered and then stared out to sea. "I'll see you later."

I took Karen up to the deck-tennis court and in a few minutes she had forgotten what William had said.

The last night out was the Captain's dinner. The Captain said Bartlett could come to it, but Bartlett refused.

I heard him tell William, "Wait until Tony Agnello does a job on this ship."

After dinner I took a stroll on the deck with Karen.

"I guess after tomorrow I'm not going to see you," I said.

"Probably not," said Karen, "but maybe when I'm a big movie star you'll come to interview me."

"Even if you're not a movie star I'll come to interview you." I put my arm around her. "I've become very fond of you," I said.

Karen pushed my arm away. "And I've become fond of you, Pete. If it hadn't been for you I don't think I could have gotten through this trip. You're a sweet boy."

"A sweet boy?" I said incredulously. "I'm a grown, hungry man."

"To me," said Karen, "you'll always be like a brother."

"Who wants to be your brother?" I said. "Karen, I'm nuts about you."

"But Pete," she said, looking at me with those innocent eyes. "I'm not nuts about you."

"There's nothing I can say to that." I said.

"Someone once told me," Karen said, "love is like chemistry. You can mix all kinds of ingredients and nothing will happen. But one day you just take two simple ingredients and poof! We're not the right chemistry, Pete."

"Name any chemical you want and I've got it."

"Yes," said Karen sadly. "But when we're together, we don't go poof."

I wanted to hit my head against the side of the boat.

Karen kissed me on the cheek and said, "Good night, Pete. I'll say good-bye to you tomorrow."

I walked around the deck for a good hour thinking about Karen, love and chemistry.

# 7

I STOPPED staring out the Hotel Excelsior window. I had to write the story of Bartlett's arrival and his exile to La Coma, Sicily. I was naturally disappointed that we weren't going to Rome or Capri or on the yacht of Bartlett's society friend, but beggers can't be choosers and neither can newspapermen. When Inspector Ruffino read that small piece of paper to Bartlett he didn't realize how he was dashing my vacation plans to bits.

But Lucas would be happy. I could just hear him say to his secretary, "Check and let me know what the hotel rates for a single room in La Coma are these days."

I wrote my story, filed it and then looked up a family my mother had asked me to see. They all wanted to go to America, and the only way I could get out was to promise I'd try my best to help them. The quota on Italian people entering the United States is filled up for the next ten years. There aren't even waiting lists because it takes so long. I thanked God, as I walked through the streets of

Naples back to the hotel, that there was no McCarran Act when my mother and father decided to come to America.

It was almost time for dinner and I went up to Karen's room to ask her if she wanted to dine with me.

I knocked on the door.

"Go away," I heard her sobbing.

"It's me, Pete," I called. "Open up."

I heard some shuffling and then Karen opened the door. Her eyes were red from crying.

"What's the matter, honey?" I asked.

"I was checking the schedules of the trains leaving for Rome tomorrow," she sniffled, "and I found an express leaving at nine in the morning. Then I got a telephone call from New York."

"Who was it?"

"I don't know. He didn't identify himself over the phone, but he said he was one of Shirley's friends. He said, 'I hear you're thinking of pulling out on the boss. You're making a big mistake.'

"I told him I didn't care and I was sorry and I'd pay them back the money as soon as I could. But he said the money didn't interest him. He said, 'I'm only concerned with the boss' happiness and if the boss has to go to Sicily then you have to go too.' He said I had made a verbal contract and that was good enough for them.

"I said I never made a verbal contract and they were thinking of Shirley. He said they didn't care what my name was; I went on the boat, so I had to stay with Bartlett.

"I told him to go to blazes and he started cursing and said, "You have a nice mother, Miss Withers, and you wouldn't want anything to happen to her.'

"I said, 'You wouldn't do anything to my mother?' and he said, 'I wouldn't, but some of the other fellows in the mob would. They're not in the habit of giving free trips away to dumb broads. You better go to Sicily for your mother's sake.' Then he hung up." Karen was in tears again.

"Don't cry," I told Karen. "I'll go down and talk to William."

I found William pressing Bartlett's suits. He was vilifying the Italian customs officials.

"What's this about making Karen go to Sicily with Bartlett?"

William said, "It's out of my hands. The boys in New York insist she goes. When the boss spoke to them before, all the boys wanted to know about was the broad. If she was everything Bartlett hoped for and stuff like that. The boss said he thought she didn't want to continue the trip and they got real sore. The boss said he didn't care if she stayed or not, but they said that wasn't the point. It cost them five grand and a contract was a contract. Bartlett said he'd leave it up to her. I guess the guys must have phoned her."

"They certainly did," I said. "William, this is tantamount to kidnaping."

"Nobody's kidnaping her," William said. "She came on the trip voluntarily. She accepted five grand in gifts and tickets. She ain't being sold into slavery. As far as I know

61

no one has laid a hand on her unless you have."

"I haven't," I said.

"So what's the beef?"

"She doesn't want to go to Sicily."

"So she don't go."

"But if she doesn't go they may do something to her mother."

"That's not my fault," William replied. "I'm not going to do anything to her mother. I don't even know her mother. Look, Pete, the original plan was to dump her as soon as we got to Naples. There are plenty of broads in Italy that are better looking than she is. But now we're going to La Coma, Sicily. We don't know what we're going to find there. I'm not going to let the boss go to La Coma in the state he's in without a broad."

"What does Bartlett say about this?" I said angrily.

"He's so mad about going to La Coma he's not giving it any thought. He's in there now talking to an Italian lawyer."

I was pretty mad too, but then I realized it would be nice to have Karen come with us to La Coma; in fact, it would be the best thing that could happen. The thought of her being there made the trip much more palatable. I guess I was just as selfish as William.

I went back to Karen's room.

"Do I have to go?" she asked anxiously.

"I'm afraid so," I said.

"Then it's true they would do things to my mother?"

"They can be pretty rough on mothers," I admitted, "Maybe because not many of them had any."

"Ohhhhhhhh," Karen said, and threw herself on the bed and cried some more.

The next evening, when I came down in the lobby with my bag to leave, I found Bartlett screaming at the room clerk, "You have no right to charge me."

"Your lawyer told us you said to pay his fee and charge it to your bill," the room clerk said.

"What's the matter?" I asked Bartlett.

"I saw some fink lawyer last night and asked him to get an injunction to stop me from going to La Coma.

"He said they couldn't send me there as it was unconstitutional. Since it was unconstitutional, I didn't need an injunction. So I said did that mean I didn't have to go? He said if the police said I did, then I had to go. He wanted three hundred bucks for this great advice and I told him to blow. So he came down here and collected from the desk clerk and they paid it without asking me. I'll be damned if I'll pay it."

Inspector Ruffino walked in at this moment.

"What's the trouble?" he asked Bartlett.

"They're trying to screw me out of a hundred and eighty-eight thousand lire."

The room clerk explained the situation.

"Better pay it, Signor Bartelini. Perhaps you can sue the lawyer later, but the hotel is not responsible."

"What if I don't?"

"Then you'll have to go down to the police station, and it will take at least two weeks before anyone listens to your story."

William came over, loaded down with baggage. "We

have to hurry if we want to make the boat," he said cheer-
fully.

"You know what they say in America, Mr. Bartlett. It's
better to pay the two dollars," I said.

Bartlett tore the bill out of the clerk's hand and threw
some money on the desk. "I'll get you too." Then he said
to William, "Let's get the hell out of here."

"We've got to wait for Karen," William said, running
after him.

"What for?"

"She's coming with us."

"I thought she didn't want to go."

"Oh, she wants to go all right."

Karen came out of the elevator in her mink coat. Her
eyes were still red. As she approached, William said,
"Karen, you're dying to go to Sicily, aren't you?"

A tear rolled down Karen's cheek. "Yeah, I'm dying to
go."

I felt like a heel as we boarded the ship for Palermo,
but in my heart of hearts, I was happy Karen was still
with us.

I met Bartlett in the lounge after the ship had left
Naples. Inspector Ruffino and his constant, uniformed
companions were sitting on the other side.

Bartlett was dressed in an immaculate tan gabardine
suit, white shirt and black tie. I thought, as I saw him, if
he were going to hell, he would have been dressed for it.

"I want you to tell the people back home," Bartlett said
"that this is a Fascist country even without Mussolini.
Tell them we're making a mistake giving them foreign

aid. They insult American citizens and have no respect for individual human rights. Our entire foreign policy has to be revised, and if you ask me, our ambassador is a fink."

"Can I quote you?" I said.

"You sure as hell can. And you can say the customs and the hotel clerks in Italy are controlled by the Communists. Apparently, word of my strongly anti-Communist record reached here before I did."

I put down everything Bartlett was saying.

"What are you going to do when you get to La Coma?"

"How do I know?" Bartlett said. "I don't even know where it is."

I pulled out a road map I had of Sicily. "I checked with the travel office in the hotel. It's marked here. The man made a cross where he thought it might be. It's between Trapani and Marsala. There's a population of about fifteen hundred people, and the main industry is tuna fishing. From Palermo the easiest way of getting there is driving through these mountains."

"What's the best hotel?" Bartlett said.

"There isn't any as far as I could find out. It's on the wrong side of the island. Most of the tourists prefer to go to Taormina and Siracusa on the other side. Don't you remember your folks talking about La Coma?"

"Maybe they did, but I never listened. La Coma never existed for me."

"I was in Sicily during the war," I told Bartlett, "but I don't think I ever went through La Coma. I covered the fighting in the mountains up above Palermo."

"Was there fighting here?" Bartlett asked.

"Pretty bad fighting," I said. "Sicily lends itself to pretty bad fighting."

It took the boat about twelve hours to get from Naples to Palermo.

In the morning I awoke early and went on deck to watch the boat pull into the Gulf of Palermo. The city itself looked far more prosperous than I had ever remembered it. There were oil tankers and large cargo ships in the harbor. Along the docks, new buildings and a hotel had been built. The rich plains above the town where the fighting I covered had taken place were now cultivated and peaceful in the morning haze. I recognized the mountains to the south and southeast. On my left was Monte Pellegrino, the Shrine of Saint Rosalia, patron of Palermo and favorite saint of all Sicilians.

The Bay of Palermo is known as the golden shell of Sicily. I remembered as a soldier how happy I was to leave it and how I vowed I would never come back. Now I was excited. Instead of the war, I remembered the wonderful fiestas, the kind and generous Sicilian people, the beautiful Sicilian girls. I remembered the shoeshine boys, the beggars, the pimps, the whores and the wine.

It would have been nice to look up some of the girls I had shacked up with, but for the life of me I couldn't think of any of their names.

## 8

WHEN we landed, we were met by a fat man in a dirty raincoat. He saluted Inspector Ruffino and the two men walked off to talk to each other. Bartlett stood looking around.

"It could be worse."

"It's not a bad city," I said. "There's plenty of action here. I wish I could remember some of their names."

Inspector Ruffino returned and introduced the fat man.

"This is Inspector Montecatini," he said. "He will take you to La Coma. I must leave you now. I hope we will have no reason to meet again."

He saluted and walked toward a waiting car.

Unlike Inspector Ruffino, Montecatini was a jovial type. He shook hands with all of us and kissed Karen's hand.

As Ruffino's car pulled out, I heard Bartlett say to William, "I think this guy can be had."

"I think you're right, boss," William said.

Bartlett said in Italian to Montecatini, "This Palermo

looks like a pretty nice town."

Montecatini smiled broadly. "It is a nice town. It is a beautiful town."

"Are you Sicilian?" Bartlett asked.

"But of course."

"I am too," said Bartlett.

"Yes, I know," said Montecatini. "You come from La Coma."

"I would love to stay in Palermo," Bartlett said.

"Ah, perhaps one day you will."

Bartlett took a hundred-dollar bill out of his pocket. "Perhaps now?"

The Inspector took the money and put it in his pocket. "Not now. Maybe later."

Bartlett gave him another hundred-dollar bill which the Inspector also pocketed. "How much later?"

Montecatini said, "When the Minister of the Interior says you no longer have to stay in La Coma."

"Better stop, boss," William said, "or he'll have your whole roll."

Bartlett said, "Well, what did he take the money for if he couldn't help us?"

Karen said, "Because you gave it to him. That's why."

A 1939 Buick drove up. "Please," said Inspector Montecatini, "it's a long drive." He opened the door.

"What about all the luggage?" William asked.

The Inspector looked at the pile of trunks. "We have no room for the trunks. Perhaps you can hire a truck and meet us there."

William looked at Bartlett. Bartlett said, "Okay. But

before you do, send Stanton another cable and tell him he's got to do something and do it fast."

William said, "Can I talk to you alone for a minute, boss?"

Bartlett looked over at Montecatini. "Of course," the Inspector said.

William and Bartlett went into a huddle.

I said to Montecatini, "Is Giuseppe Mondello still operating in these parts?"

Montecatini smiled. "All you Americans want to know about Giuseppe Mondello."

"I don't," said Karen. "Who is Giuseppe Mondello?"

I told Karen, "He's Sicily's most famous bandit."

Montecatini said, "He is glamourized far out of proportion to his profession. Mondello is a myth created by newspapermen."

Bartlett came back and we all piled into the Buick. Montecatini sat next to the driver, Bartlett, Karen and I in the back. We left William behind to find a truck.

Karen said, "Can we go sightseeing?"

"I'm awfully sorry," Montecatini said, "but it is a long drive and we must get to La Coma."

"I'll show you Palermo sometime, Karen," I offered.

Bartlett seemed annoyed. "You're getting to be quite the American Express guide."

"I'm sorry, Mr. Bartlett," I said. "I'm just a tourist at heart."

"That's a promise, Pete," Karen said. "And I'm going to hold you to it."

We started off with a roar.

The Buick sped madly through the streets of Palermo, the driver pressing his foot on the accelerator and his hand on the horn. In twenty minutes we were out of the city, climbing up into the mountains. The driver seemed determined to break a speed record from Palermo to La Coma.

Karen said to Bartlett, "Can't you make him slow down?"

"I remember during the war," I said, "Sicilian traffic even then was the most dangerous in the world. The members of the Mafia are Boy Scouts compared to the people who own drivers' licenses in Sicily."

Our driver was cursing a truck in front of him and waving both hands in anger.

"He doesn't have a hand on the wheel!" Bartlett said in amazement.

"They can't curse each other," I told him, "unless they have both hands free. That's what causes the accidents."

Our driver finally passed the truck on a curve. When he got the car straightened out he looked back and cursed some more. The driver of the truck also had both his hands off the wheel and was moving his mouth in curses.

Karen, by this time, had her hands over her eyes.

"Tell him to slow down," Bartlett said to Montecatini. Montecatini said, "I could not do that. If he slowed down, he would feel he was a coward and a disgrace to his entire family. Nothing will slow him down except a donkey cart."

A few miles later, the car was slowed down by a donkey cart. The driver blew his horn furiously, but the donkey cart owner paid no attention.

"Notice," I said to Bartlett, "the paintings on the cart.

Everyone paints his donkey cart with stories of either knights or miracles. The braces of the cart are hand carved."

"Who cares?" Bartlett said. "I don't want to look at paintings all day."

Montecatini said, "It is my guess that the driver is asleep and so is the donkey."

Behind us, other cars piled up and blew their horns. Sicilians all the way down the line were screaming at each other and waving their hands. But only when the cart turned off the road, fifteen minutes later, could anyone resume normal speed.

We drove through rich farmland with olive trees and grape orchards, and then we climbed again only to find a wilderness of rocks and cactus. It was dusty and hot and we closed the windows to keep out the dust, which made it even hotter. Karen had taken off her fur coat.

"Oh, why," she said, "did I have to wear a suit?"

In about an hour we were the only ones on the road.

Suddenly, up ahead, we saw a large hay wagon stuck in the middle of the road. There was no room for the Buick to pass, and the car came to a screeching halt, almost crashing into the wagon's rear end.

Montecatini, the driver, Bartlett and I got out of the car to see what was going on. As we walked toward the wagon, three men with handkerchiefs over their faces jumped out from behind the clump of bushes, each with a submachine gun in his hand.

Montecatini froze in his tracks. "It's Giuseppe Mondello."

"Hello, Inspector," said the tallest of the men in Italian. "I didn't expect to see you."

Montecatini said apologetically, "I obviously didn't expect to see you. My mission is to take him back to La Coma."

"It doesn't matter. We won't bother you. Everyone put his hands up."

"Are you Bartelini?" Mondello came up and asked me.

"Hell, no." I said.

"I'm Bartelini," Bartlett said. "Who wants to know?"

Mondello went over to him. "Me, Giuseppe Mondello."

"You punk," Bartlett said.

Mondello slapped Bartlett across the face hard and Bartlett's lip started bleeding.

Karen screamed and got out of the car.

Mondello wheeled around. "Who's she?"

Nobody said anything.

Karen didn't know what to do so she walked up to Mondello and whipped out her passport.

"I'm an American. If you do bad things to us, my government will drop an atom bomb on you."

She made her hands into a plane and went, "Bzzzzz booom."

Mondello shook his head in confusion. He took Karen's passport and looked at it. Then he smiled. "American? You, American?"

Karen nodded.

Mondello turned to Montecatini and said, "Tell her I am Giuseppe Mondello and I want to make Sicily the forty-ninth state. I have just written the President of the

72

United States and I am waiting for a reply."

Montecatini translated and Karen said, "Tell him it's a heck of a way to spend his time waiting."

One of the other bandits urged Mondello to hurry, and the three men went immediately into action. Mondello searched Bartlett and took his wallet and his wrist watch. But when he went through the wallet, he seemed disappointed. There were only a few hundred dollars in it.

Mondello came over to me and started searching but Montecatini said, "He's an American also."

Mondello looked at my passport and cursed but he stopped searching. He went over to the Buick and looked in the front and back seats. He picked up Karen's vanity case and was just about to open it when Karen went over and said, "Hey, that's my bag."

Mondello opened it anyway, looked through it and closed it in disappointment. He threw the bag back on the seat and was going to open the trunk when one of his henchmen shouted that a truck was coming.

Mondello aimed his machine gun at us and said, "Don't anyone move for ten minutes. I'm sorry I had to bother you, Inspector."

"It was no bother," Montecatini said.

Mondello bowed to Karen and said, "God bless the mother who bore you."

I translated and Karen smiled, "Why, thank you."

Mondello snapped at Bartlett, "You don't deserve such a beautiful girl. If she wasn't an American, I'd ask her to come with me."

Bartlett said, "You cheap hood."

Mondello was going to slap Bartlett again when one of his men whistled and they all disappeared over the hill.

"Are you going after them?" Bartlett yelled at the Inspector.

"They have horses, and besides there isn't much you can do in Mondello country."

"What kind of a police officer are you," Bartlett said, "if you can't protect someone in the same car you're driving in?"

"It really isn't my territory," Montecatini protested.

By this time the truck had pulled up behind us and the driver was blowing his horn.

Montecatini was mad by now and he went over and told the driver to stop honking his horn. The driver yelled back savagely and the Inspector walked away. "No one," he said, "has any respect for the law any more."

We all got back into the Buick after the driver and the truck driver pushed the hay wagon off the road.

Karen took a handkerchief out of her pocket and said, "The nasty man cut you."

"It's just a scratch," Bartlett said.

Karen licked her handkerchief and wiped Bartlett's mouth. "If there's anything I hate," she said, "it's a bully."

"What about my wallet?" Bartlett said to the Inspector. "I had a lot of important papers in it."

"Maybe we'll find it," Montecatini said, "but it's doubtful. You're very lucky, as he usually takes people's pants."

"Doesn't a private citizen have any protection in this country?" Bartlett asked.

"Oh, yes," said the Inspector. "You'll find out about that later."

"So that's Giuseppe Mondello," I said. "Man, what a scoop."

Montecatini said, "Mondello isn't a bad sort. He never robs the police or tourists. That is much in his favor. He is what you might call our Robin Hood."

"Hoodlum's a better word," Bartlett said.

"If everyone knows who he is," Karen said, "why does he wear a handkerchief over his face?"

"They tell me," the Inspector said, "he's a great fan of American cowboy pictures. He takes his role seriously."

"Why don't the police arrest him?"

"That's a hard question to answer. First, we can never find him when we have enough men. The villagers and mountain people will never give us any information.

"Secondly, he is a friend of the Mafia, and it would be impossible in these parts to offend anyone who is a friend of the Mafia. Incidentally, he was born in La Coma also, Mr. Bartelini."

Bartlett said, "He's got some pretty good intelligence. He knew exactly when we were coming and even what road we were taking."

"Mr. Bartelini, you will find out in this part of the world there are no secrets and everything is a secret."

"I still don't understand how a guy like that can move around scot free."

"Perhaps," said Montecatini, "he has the right connections. Surely a man like you can understand that."

Karen said, "Wait until I write Shirley about this."

# 9

WE STOPPED for lunch in a café in a small village. There were flies on everything and only the Inspector and the chauffeur could eat the food. I had forgotten about the flies of Sicily but suddenly it all came back to me in one great flood of nausea. Bartlett, Karen and I drank beer. Bartlett's tan suit was pretty wrinkled by now. I had taken off my tie, but he refused to take off his.

We got back in the Buick and rode for two more hours. Occasionally we passed a small village or a monastery, but the country itself was bare of all human life.

"How much further is it?" Bartlett asked.

The Inspector said, "You will be able to see it as soon as we get around this bend."

When the car turned the bend we saw the sea, and far down below what looked to be a tiny fishing village with fishing boats anchored idly in a small cove.

"That," said the Inspector, "is La Coma. It is very beautiful from up here. La Coma is a very old town even by Sicilian standards. There is an ancient Roman theater above the town and you can occasionally find some interesting antiquities."

It took us an hour to descend to the sea. As we neared the town, shepherds waved at us and we passed donkey carts and horse-drawn wagons with people who looked very dressed up for Sicilians on a weekday.

La Coma was built in a crescent shape on a hill, and, as we approached, the white stone houses seemed to be sitting right on top of each other. I saw a church steeple in what was apparently the center of town, but it was tilted on a crazy angle, and it was partly destroyed. Overlooking La Coma at its highest point was a forbidding castle with two large fortress towers. There were ancient cannons sticking out from the towers and they looked as if they were ready to fire on the town.

As we entered the town we saw children shouting, waving and cheering us. In the distance we heard a band. When we drove down the narrow street we saw people in the windows waving to us and there were American flags hanging from many of the balconies.

"What's going on?" I said.

Karen said, "It looks like they're celebrating the Fourth of July."

Just before we arrived at the town square, we saw a large banner strung across the street which said in Italian, "Welcome to Frank Bartelini, La Coma's Most Famous Son."

Hundreds of people were gathered in the square. On a stand in front of the town hall, a band was sitting. When the people saw our car, they rushed toward us and the band broke into a Sicilian version of "The Star-Spangled Banner."

I grabbed my camera and jumped out of the car to take pictures. Bartlett was half lifted and half dragged out of the car. He was looking around in bewilderment when an old lady threw her arms around him and cried, "Francesco, Francesco!"

Bartlett tried to push her away. "Who are you?" He had to shout.

"I am your Aunt Gabriella," she said. "And these are your cousins: Pilade, Eduardo, Maria, Gina and Gisella."

As each one was introduced he or she smothered Bartlett with kisses, except for Gisella, who appeared to be the eldest. She just stared coldly.

Karen got out of the car and the people cheered.

"What are they cheering me for?" Karen asked.

"They think you're his wife," I said.

"Well, tell them I'm not."

I told them and the women started murmuring and a few screamed at their husbands for leering at Karen.

The band broke into "It's a Long Way to Tipperary," and Bartlett was dragged by several men to the shaky rostrum. A man with a red sash across his shiny navy-blue suit helped him up in front of the band. I asked who the man with the ribbon was and a man told me it was the Mayor of La Coma. The Mayor raised his hand for silence and the band stopped in the middle of the song. Then the Mayor took a piece of paper out of his pocket and started to read.

"Citizens of La Coma, honored guests," he nodded toward where Karen and I were standing, "and friends. Today is a great day in the life of our little town. One of our great sons, who left La Coma as a baby, has seen fit to leave the great country of the United States of America and return to the land of his birth."

There were cheers and applause.

"We, who knew and loved his parents, are aware of the sacrifices he has made to come back to us and we want him to know La Coma's hearts are open to him."

The people nodded their heads.

"Before he went to America, no one ever heard of La Coma. But now, thanks to him, people all over know that La Coma can produce men like Frank Bartelini."

More cheers.

"In the U.S.A., Frank Bartelini was a powerful and rich man. We hope he will show us the way to prosperity and make La Coma as happy as he made the United States of America."

A man jumped on the platform and shouted "Viva Bartelini!"

The Mayor kissed Bartlett on both cheeks and indicated he was to make a speech.

I pushed through the crowd to get a better photo of the event.

Bartlett finally said, "I want to thank you for the wonderful reception you have given me. Although I have been in America these many years, I want you to know my thoughts have always been in La Coma. I couldn't wait to return."

There was some applause.

"I can't tell how long I'm going to be here, but I want you to know that I'm happy to be among so many friends and when I get back to the United States of America I'm going to try to get you a loan."

Cheers.

"I'm sorry my mother and father can't be with me on this occasion, but I know they're looking down from Heaven and smiling on all of you."

Bartlett's aunt sobbed.

"I'm so overcome I don't have any more to say."

Karen pushed through to where I was standing. She said, as the Mayor kissed Bartlett again, "He sounds like he's running for office."

Suddenly two men lifted Karen up onto the platform.

The Mayor said, "Not only has Mr. Bartelini come back to La Coma, but he has brought a beautiful woman with him."

The men cheered and applauded wildly while the women stared curiously at Karen's clothes.

Karen screamed at me, "What should I do?"

"Say something," I yelled.

Karen looked out at all the people and said, "I want a bath."

The Mayor translated and everyone laughed and clapped.

Montecatini went over to the platform and shouted something up to the Mayor. The Mayor bent over and Montecatini talked to him. Then the Mayor raised his hand again for silence.

"And also we have with us tonight a most distinguished American journalist who has come all the way from the United States of America to write about La Coma and its great son, Frank Bartelini."

The two men who lifted Karen on the platform now lifted me up there.

I looked around at Karen and Bartlett. "What am I supposed to do?"

"Say something," said Karen, laughing.

"Honored friends of La Coma," I began. "My newspaper has asked me to come here to write the true story of Frank Bartelini. They believe that here in La Coma I will find many answers to the questions that Americans have been asking about Frank Bartelini for years. I am happy to be here on this day of welcome and I assure you if anyone can bring prosperity to La Coma, it's Mr. Bartelini."

I got a big hand.

"You're laying it on kind of thick, aren't you?" Bartlett said.

"No more than anyone else is here today."

Bartlett said to the Mayor, "Thanks a lot. Now we'd like to get some sleep."

"But," protested the Mayor, "you cannot go. We're having a fiesta for you. All these people have come to see you. They have put on their best clothes and have made special food. You cannot leave now."

Three chairs were produced for us and we sat down in front of the band, looking out at the people.

Long tables were set up on all sides of the square and from each of the houses women and children brought out large platters of steaming food.

The band began to play Sicilian dance music and the Mayor came over to Bartlett and said, "Would you care to dance?"

"With whom?" Bartlett asked.

"With me," the Mayor replied.

"You're kidding," Bartlett said.

"No," said the Mayor, smiling. "In our village the men dance with each other and the women dance with each other. The priest forbids mixed dancing."

Bartlett shook his head. "Not for me. Thanks."

The Mayor said, "If you don't start they won't be able to dance." He pulled Bartlett off his chair and helped him down off the platform. The crowd made room for them and the two men started dancing as the villagers clapped their hands. I was busy snapping photos.

Bartlett's aunt came to the platform and indicated she wanted to dance with Karen. Two men helped Karen down and she was off with the aunt, dancing in a whirl.

A big fisherman grabbed me next and I found myself being thrown around the square. I held my camera with one hand and danced with the other. Once Karen went by and screamed, "Help me!"

"I can't," I said. "I can't help myself."

A few minutes later I found myself in Bartlett's arms. "You promised me the first dance," I said.

Bartlett said, "Wise guy!" as I threw him over to the big fisherman.

The party was in full swing as the wine bottles were passed around, lanterns were turned on, and the band, which never seemed to get tired, played on and on.

At last they stopped and we were led over to one of the tables, where the three of us collapsed in chairs. Bartlett finally took off his tie. He was puffing and wheezing.

I thought Karen was going to faint. I picked up a bottle of wine and took a long drink. I passed it to Karen, who also took a drink. Then the big fisherman staggered over, took the bottle to his mouth, and, after taking a drink, wiped it with a dirty scarf and passed it to Bartlett. Bartlett shook his head but the fisherman urged him to drink up. Bartlett gulped and took a swallow. Then he went green. I helped him as he rushed behind the church and retched.

"This is a pretty lively town," I said.

Color was coming back in Bartlett's face. "You seem to be enjoying the whole thing."

"What the hell," I said. "Why fight it? I may be here for a month." I almost added, "And you may be here for longer than that."

I led Bartlett back to the head of the table. More food had been brought out. Steaming bowls of rice and snails, large chunks of pork, cakes of all kinds. The people who weren't dancing were eating and singing.

The Mayor was forcing the rice and snails on Bartlett, who was looking green again.

"You don't look well," Karen said.

"I'll be all right."

"Have a little more wine."

Bartlett went behind the church again.

The party lasted into the night. It reached its pitch

around ten o'clock. Just as the excitement was at its height, two tall Sicilians walked into the square carrying shotguns under their arms.

A woman screamed and everyone became quiet.

Bartlett's aunt rushed over to him. "It's the Frasconi brothers."

"Who are the Frasconi brothers?" he asked.

His aunt didn't have time to reply.

The brothers came over to our table and one of them tapped Bartlett on the shoulder with his shotgun.

Bartlett said, "What do you think you're doing?"

The Mayor stood up. "You boys get out of here. You're spoiling the party."

The brothers didn't bother to look at the Mayor. "Bartelini," one of them said, "your grandfather and our grandfather had a vendetta. Your father and our father had a vendetta. We want to continue the vendetta. Are you in agreement?"

"Yes, he is," screamed the aunt. "The Frasconis are pigs. His grandfather said you were pigs, his father said you were pigs and now he will tell you that you are pigs. Tell them, Francesco."

"Tell them what?"

"Tell them they are pigs."

"Why?"

"So you can continue the vendetta."

"But I don't want to get into a vendetta," Bartlett said.

"You have to," his aunt said. "You're the only Bartelini left. You will disgrace all of us if you do not continue the vendetta, and the people of the town will think you are afraid of the Frasconis."

"What is your answer, grandson of a pig?" a Frasconi said.

"My grandfather said you were pigs?"

"Yes."

"And my father said you were pigs?"

"Yes."

"Then," said Bartlett, looking helplessly at his aunt, "I guess you are pigs."

The brothers raised their shotguns, but several of the men in the square grabbed them before they could fire.

"Not tonight," the Mayor said, raising his hand. "No vendettas tonight."

The men dragged the Frasconi brothers, who were screaming oaths, out of the square.

Bartlett's aunt kissed him. "We've been waiting all these years for you to avenge the wrongs the Frasconis committed against our families."

Bartlett was very shaken.

"What is the vendetta about?"

"Nobody can remember," his aunt replied. "But you can be sure your grandfather started it for a good reason."

"Why haven't your sons been part of the vendetta?"

"I was your father's sister. We are not Bartelinis. It is always the eldest son who must lead the vendetta."

I told Karen what had happened.

"I thought vendettas only happened in the Blue Ridge Mountains of Virginia."

"No," I said, "Sicily is the grandmother of the vendetta.

They take them quite seriously. One or the other family must be eliminated before the wrong has been righted."

Karen shook her head sadly. "How can one girl get into so much trouble so fast?"

The Frasconi brothers had thrown cold water on the party and pretty soon people started to go home.

Karen called over to Bartlett, "Hey, hero, where are we going to sleep tonight?"

Bartlett asked the Mayor where the hotel was.

The Mayor pointed to a café. "Vincent has a few rooms to rent to tourists."

Karen said, "Where is my make-up kit?"

"I'll get it," said Bartlett, walking over to the Buick.

Karen went with him to get her mink coat.

When they came back I said, "Where is William?"

Bartlett said, "He should have been here by now."

The Mayor took us over to Vincent's café, and Vincent, a grinning fat proprietor, led us up two flights of creaky stairs. He said, between puffs, "You are lucky. This is the finest hotel in La Coma."

He opened the door to a dark dingy room with a double bed and an armchair. The bedspread was torn and the wallpaper had rainspots all over it. When Vincent turned on the light, several flies buzzed around the room.

"You got the Presidential suite," I told Karen.

Bartlett said, "Is this the best you've got?"

Vincent replied, "It's the best room in La Coma."

Bartlett said, "Now we want two more rooms."

"I do not have two more rooms," Vincent said sadly. "I have only one more room."

"Does it have two beds?" Bartlett asked.

"No. Just one."

"Maybe I could stay here?" I suggested.

"Oh no, you don't," said Karen.

"All right. You can have the bed, Mr. Bartlett," I said. "After all it's your deportation. I'll sleep on the floor."

"Let's see how big the bed is," Bartlett said. "I'm so sleepy it doesn't make any difference to me."

"Me neither," I said. "I always say you don't really know a man until you've slept with him."

Vincent had disappeared down the hall and Bartlett opened Karen's vanity case on her bed.

"Hey, what are you doing?" Karen cried.

Bartlett was searching through the vanity case.

He didn't find what he was looking for. "All right, sister, where is it?"

"What?" Karen said.

"The money belt. William put it in your vanity case for safekeeping when we left Palermo. Come on. Cough it up."

"Mondello opened the vanity case," I said.

"Come on," said Bartlett, grabbing her arm roughly. "I don't like dames pulling tricks."

Karen reddened and broke away. "You big oaf. I found the money belt in my vanity case when you got out of the car. I hid it in the lining of my mink coat so Mondello wouldn't find it. How dare you accuse me of stealing your money?"

Karen went over to her mink coat, took out the money belt and threw it at Bartlett. "Now get out," she cried, "and go to the devil."

Bartlett was embarrassed. "Karen, I'm . . . sorry. I just didn't realize . . ."

"Get out. I don't want your apologies. I just want to get some sleep."

She pushed both of us out the door and slammed it shut.

"I guess I goofed on that one," Bartlett said sadly, holding the money belt.

"The trouble with you, Mr. Bartlett, if you don't mind my saying so, is you don't trust people."

"Who the hell asked you?"

We found Vincent down the hall making up a double bed. The room was slightly smaller and the worse for wear.

We undressed in silence.

"Which side do you want?"

"I don't care," he said.

"It's your homecoming," I said. "You should at least have that choice."

Bartlett lay down in one side of the bed and I sank down on the other. I switched off the light.

We lay in silence for a few minutes and then I said, "Mr. Bartlett?"

"Yeah?"

"Now that we're sleeping together, could I call you Frank?"

"Yeah, Pete. Call me Frank."

"Thanks, Frank."

I rolled over and went right to sleep.

# 10

BARTLETT was dressing by the time I woke up the next morning.

"How did you sleep?" I asked him.

"Not so good."

"I was out like a light."

"I couldn't sleep. I felt like a heel accusing Karen of stealing my dough. That was a pretty rotten thing to do on my part."

"Too bad there's not a jewelry store in town," I said. "You could go down and buy her a gift."

"Yeah," said Bartlett. "Maybe I'll send William in to Palermo to buy her something."

I started whistling, "Diamonds Are a Girl's Best Friend."

Bartlett was dressed now. I guess I had gone a little too far because he whirled around and said, "Look, sonny, I'm getting tired of your wisecracks. I've been pretty nice to you, but you're getting on my nerves. I don't want any more remarks about the girl, and keep your hands off her."

"I haven't touched her, Frank, honestly I haven't. And I promise . . . no more wisecracks."

Bartlett went over to the window and looked out on the empty square. "I wonder if William got in last night?"

He went downstairs and I joined him for coffee. It was my first chance to really see La Coma. The square had been mysteriously cleaned up from last night's party and looked very neat. Except for a group of children playing in the square, nobody was around although it was nine o'clock in the morning. Vincent's café and hotel took up one side of the square. On the left of the café was the post office, and on the right, the town hall where the bandstand had been set up last night. Facing us, with the crazy steeple, was the church.

Below the church were cobblestoned streets which dipped sharply down four blocks to the pier. Above were the houses. And above the houses, the forbidding castle.

An occasional truck or car drove through the town, its horn honking loudly to frighten everyone off the street. But from where we sat, it seemed there were no cars in the town itself. What little local traffic there was consisted of donkey carts and perhaps one or two motor scooters.

Bartlett was still wearing his tan gabardine suit, which was now not only wrinkled but dirty. He was cursing William.

"Where the hell could he possibly be?"

"I don't know. But I sure would love a clean shirt and a pair of clean socks."

"We've got to find ourselves different quarters. I'm

*90*

not going to sleep in this joint another night."

The Mayor came by and bowed. We asked him to join us for coffee.

"How did you sleep?" he asked.

"Lousy," Bartlett said. "Isn't there any other hotel in town?"

The Mayor said regretfully, "Unfortunately this is the only hotel. You are not the first ones to complain. Perhaps if we had a better hotel we could get tourists to stop here."

"Aren't there any rooms to be rented?"

"The only extra rooms in this town are in the del Grandi castle, up there on the hill."

"Who owns it?" Bartlett asked.

"Didn't your parents ever tell you about the del Grandis?" the Mayor said in a surprised voice.

"I don't remember if they did or not."

"The castle is owned by the Principessa del Grandi. She also owns all the good farm land around here and the tuna-fishing rights. The del Grandis have lived here for eight hundred years. They have left their mark on La Coma, no one will dispute that."

"This Principessa, what kind of woman is she?"

"Old and bitter, like a dried-up olive. She must be over eighty years old and the only thing that keeps her alive is avarice. Her one dream is to starve the servants to death so she will outlive them."

"Does she live alone there?"

"No. She lives with her idiot son. The del Grandis never seem to be able to produce worthwhile male heirs. The women have always been the strong ones in the family.

When a del Grandi woman marries, she makes her husband take the del Grandi name. The Principessa is mad, but everyone in La Coma is afraid of her."

"And you say she has extra bedrooms?"

"Maybe fifty. But I don't know if she would rent them. Yet she likes money very much and it's entirely possible, if you're willing to pay . . ."

"I'm willing to pay," Bartlett said. "Anything to get out of this hole."

"Vincent is going to be very hurt," the Mayor said.

"I'll keep a room here just for a guest," Bartlett said.

"Whom are you expecting?" I asked Bartlett.

"Maybe the Minister of the Interior will come visit me," he said sarcastically.

Karen came downstairs. She didn't look so good in the morning. There were circles under her eyes, and she was wearing the suit she had on the day before.

"There is nothing," she said, crumbling into a chair, "nothing or nobody that's going to make me spend another night in that room."

"That's exactly what we were saying," I said to Karen. "I'm going to report Vincent to the Hotel Association."

Vincent brought Karen a muddy cup of coffee.

Suddenly we saw a man coming across the square. He had nothing on but his underwear.

"It's William," Bartlett shouted.

The three of us rushed over to him.

"What happened?" Bartlett demanded.

"Let me sit down first," William begged.

Bartlett and I half carried him over to a chair and sat

him down. Bartlett yelled to Vincent to bring some coffee.

"Tell us what happened," he said.

"Bandits," William blurted out. "Hijackers. They took the truck, they stole the trunks, they took my gun, my clothes . . . everything. There must have been fifty of them."

"There were probably only three," Bartlett said.

"How did you know?" William asked in surprise.

"Did they take my clothes too?" Karen cried.

"They took everything."

"But didn't you tell them I was an American citizen?"

William said, "I didn't tell them anything."

"Oh," said Karen, "my clothes, my boat ticket, everything . . . gone."

"My suits, my shirts, my underwear," said Bartlett, "and my golf clubs."

"The paper will never believe me," I said.

By this time the children in the square were screaming and pointing at William. Their mothers came out and started screaming also.

Inspector Montecatini hurried down the street with his chauffeur. "What's going on?"

"He met up with your friend Mondello," Bartlett said. "The son-of-a-bitch stole all our trunks."

Montecatini was outraged. "Look at him! He can't sit there like that in his underwear."

"The hell with his underwear . . . ! What about our trunks?"

"First things first," Montecatini said. "This is a very

serious situation. It is scandalous for the children. Take him inside."

Bartlett and I took William into the café.

Montecatini said sternly, "I'm going to have to fine him."

"For what?" I asked.

"Indecent exposure. It's a very serious offense in these parts."

"What about the theft?"

"We'll make a report," Montecatini promised. "But robbery is one thing, indecent exposure is another. One can understand being robbed, but it is very difficult to explain why someone walks around in his underwear."

Bartlett held his head in his hands. "I'm going out of my mind."

Vincent brought a pair of coveralls for William.

When he was no longer indecently exposed, and had paid the fine, we decided the first thing was to go up and see the Principessa about renting the rooms. It was a long steep climb, taking us almost a half hour. Neither Karen nor Bartlett had the right shoes for climbing La Coma's cobbled streets. We were all out of breath by the time we reached the rusted gate of the castle. There was a large sign hanging askew from the gate which said: PRIVATE PROPERTY. ANYONE WHO ENTERS WILL BE SHOT.

A caretaker's house stood next to the gate, but it looked as if it hadn't been lived in for years. As we entered the property we were lost in a tangle of weeds, wild growth, rotted trees and stagnant pools of water. We followed a twisted dirt road alternately full of rocks and deep holes.

The castle loomed up in front of us. It looked even larger than it did from down below. The sides were covered with vines and moss. Around the castle was a moat. The drawbridge to the large wooden door at the entrance was down.

Karen stared and said, "It's something out of the twelfth century."

"It looks older than that to me," I said.

We crossed the drawbridge, hesitantly waiting for someone to fire a gun. I found a long rope and pulled it. It rang a bell at the top of the castle.

Soon an old butler, dressed in knee pants, tails, dirty white collar and white tie, opened the door. He looked out at us with suspicion.

I explained we wanted to see the Principessa del Grandi. He hesitated a minute and then let us in. He indicated we should wait in the hall, and he walked away up a long winding staircase. The interior of the castle, if not clean, was at least cool, and the four of us sank onto the bench in the hall.

The butler returned in ten minutes and told us to follow him.

We found the Principessa sitting behind her desk in the bedroom. She was poring over some accounting books and did not bother to look up when we came in. If she didn't look eighty, she at least looked seventy-nine. Her hair was dyed black, her thin butchered face was covered with wrinkles, and when she finally did look up, we found ourselves staring into bitter, fierce eyes that moved quickly back and forth studying our faces.

The first words she said were, "What are you doing on my property?"

Bartlett spoke up. "We wanted to talk to you about renting a room. My name is . . ."

"I know what your name is," the Principessa spat back. "I knew your grandfather and I knew your father. Wastrels, both of them. Never did give me an honest day's work."

I saw Bartlett's face redden. I kicked him and decided to take up the ball. "Principessa, I'm an American journalist and this man," pointing to William, "is Mr. Bartlett's valet. This young lady is our friend."

The Principessa stood up and looked Karen over. "One of those wild American girls?"

Bartlett said, "I don't care what your opinion of me is, but don't make any remarks about the girl. She isn't what you think she is."

The Principessa said, "How do you know what I think she is? Now, what do you want?"

"We want," I said as diplomatically as possible, "to rent rooms for a week or two."

"Never!" the Principessa said. "A Bartelini never slept in this house and he never will. I would not let one sleep in the stable."

"How much do you want for the rooms?" Bartlett said, taking a roll of American bills out of his pocket.

A glint came into the Principessa's eyes as she stared at the money. "Two hundred dollars a week," she said hesitatingly.

When Bartlett didn't flinch and threw the money on the

96

table, she seemed disappointed she hadn't asked for more.

"That doesn't include meals or clean towels," she added.

"I guessed that," Bartlett said.

The Principessa clutched the money and put it into her dress. "We eat at one sharp and seven in the evening. I'll rent the rooms on a temporary basis. You can have three rooms. The girl is in one by herself and I don't care how the others divide up. But no monkey business with the girl."

Bartlett said to me in English, "I'd love to slug her in the kisser."

The Principessa cackled, "I also speak English."

She said, "Alfredo will show you to your rooms." She turned her back on us.

Karen whispered to me as we were leaving, "What was that all about?"

"The Principessa questioned your virtue and Bartlett got mad," I said.

"I would never have believed it," Karen said. "Not in a million years."

It was decided that William and I would share the third room together. Fortunately there were two beds. There was no discussion about closet space or drawers since neither of us had any clothing. The room was immense— quite a change from the one I had shared on the previous night.

Since my typewriter had also been stolen, I had to write my stories out in longhand. It was a tough, torturous process. I wrote up our encounter with Mondello on the highway. I decided to spread out the stories. I planned to

97

file Bartlett's arrival in La Coma and the holdup of William the next day separately. There was no sense incorporating all of it in one article. Besides, if I did, no one would believe me. Using paper I stole from a desk in the Principessa's living room and a pencil I found in a drawer, I went to work. I finished about 12:30 and rushed down to the post office. It was closed until three o'clock for lunch. I had to hike all the way back up to the castle.

When I returned, everyone was seated at the table, except William, who was out trying to buy us some clothes.

The dining room was a long hall that had fed del Grandis for centuries. But not too well, if the portraits on the wall were true studies of the ancestors. They were all women. There must have been twenty of them and they all looked like the Principessa.

There was one tremendous oil over the Principessa's head showing an ancient Principessa standing on a balcony of the castle with her dress held high and nothing underneath. She seemed to be shouting something. I thought at the time it was a very odd painting.

Alfredo, the old servant, served a tepid, oily fish soup.

The Principessa, who had Karen on her right, said to her, "Are you going to marry that man down there?"

"Not even if they kill my mother," Karen said.

"You look like a very healthy girl. You seem to have strong legs."

"I was a dancer," Karen said.

"Do you know anything about tuna?" the Principessa said.

"Only that it comes out of a can."

"You American girls . . . yet one could learn. I learned."

Alfredo served a large bowl of spaghetti in which could be found, if one searched carefully, a few pieces of chicken.

"My son isn't much to look at."

No one at the table gave her an argument.

"But the woman who marries him would inherit not only this castle, the land, but also all the tuna-fishing rights in La Coma."

Bartlett smiled at Karen. "It sounds like a wonderful opportunity for any girl."

"Women have always run this family," the old Principessa continued. "Do you see that painting behind me? That was the second Principessa del Grandi, who ruled in the fourteenth century, the greatest Principessa of us all. She waged wars on neighboring dukes, robbed the King's caravans with her henchmen, sank ships of friendly nations who dared approach her waters, and poached on everybody's fishing territories. She had no use for the wretched filthy peasants who lived in La Coma, and she treated them with contempt and," the old lady cackled, "to a few tortures also. One day, the rabble kidnaped three of her children. They gathered out there across the moat and held the children over their heads. 'Come out, you whore,' they screamed, 'or we'll slay your children in front of your eyes.'"

The Principessa looked as if she were reliving the scene.

"The bitch came out all right. She stood on the balcony of her bedroom and she lifted her skirts as you see in that painting. Then, pointing to the lower part of her body, she screamed at them, 'Kill them if you want to! I still have what it takes to make a lot more!' "

"What happened to the children?" I asked.

"The mob killed them. But, true to her promise, she made a lot more."

"I could never do that," Karen shuddered.

"That's what it takes to make a Principessa in Sicily," the old lady said.

The food hadn't been very good but at least there were no flies on it, and once we had become accustomed to Alfredo's dirty gloves, we could eat it.

At lunch, Karen had told the Principessa about her trunks being stolen and the Principessa offered to lend her some clothes. She took Karen upstairs to dig through an old trunk.

Bartlett said he was going to take a nap, and I wandered back into town to wait until the post office opened.

I met William climbing up the hill with two large packages under his arm. "I bought out the whole store," he said, puffing. "I got you some duds. They're surplus U.S. Army officers' clothes but they're better than nothing. They didn't have anything for Karen."

I told William I'd be back after I filed my story.

The post office finally opened and the postmaster, grumbling about not getting any sleep, took my story.

I told him I wanted to cable it collect.

He had never seen such a long telegram and he couldn't believe I wanted to send it by cable. Then I showed him my collect Italian Post Office credit card. He had never seen one and said he'd have to wire to Palermo for instructions.

I hung around for two hours waiting for Palermo to reply.

Palermo replied. They had to check with Rome.

That is why the first story on Mondello robbing Bartlett appeared in the *News-Press* two days after it happened.

It didn't mean that I wasn't receiving any word from the *News-Press*.

That evening a telegram arrived from Simpson: SENDING THIS TO ROME, NAPLES, PALERMO AND LA COMA. WHERE ARE YOU AND WHY HAVEN'T YOU FOLLOWED UP FIRST STORY.

I sent Simpson a reply the next day: AM IN LA COMA, YOUR CREDIT CARD BEING QUESTIONED. HAVE FILED AND YOU SHOULD BE RECEIVING SOONEST. PETE.

The day the story of the Mondello robbery was printed in the *News-Press*, Simpson cabled: YOUR STORY ON BART-LETT STICKUP PAGE ONE HERE. AP PICKED UP AND SENT OUT ALL OVER COUNTRY WITH CREDIT TO US. CAN YOU SEND MORE.

I sent the second story of Bartlett's reception in La Coma and received another Simpson cable: GREAT STORY. AP AGAIN PICKING UP. GIVE US MORE ON FRASCONI VENDETTA. IT HAS ALL OF NEW YORK LAUGHING. LUCAS AND BOYLE DE-LIGHTED.

I filed the third story of William getting held up and all the trunks being stolen.

This time Simpson wasn't as elated: ARE YOU SURE YOU NOT MAKING THIS ALL UP. IT SOUNDS MORE LIKE WILD WEST THAN SICILY. BETTER GET OFF THE WINE AND DOWN TO WORK. SIMPSON.

I knew they wouldn't believe the third story and I cursed myself for sending it.

Bartlett was also getting cables. The La Coma post office

hadn't been so busy for years.

William told me in our bedroom, "All hell's breaking loose in New York. Rizzolli is making a big pitch at taking over the mob.

"Somehow he found out the boss was sent to La Coma and about Mondello sticking us up. He's told the guys in our organization that the boss isn't coming back. Tommy is pretty upset because he doesn't think he can keep the gang together if the boss doesn't get back real soon."

"What's Bartlett going to do about it?"

"He's placed a call through to Tommy but God knows when he's going to get it."

# 11

It was surprising how, in a few days, we all settled down to a routine. Bartlett, William and I were dressed in khaki officers' uniforms, without the insignia, of course. True to form, Bartlett wore an officers' tie and William made sure his pants were pressed and cleaned every day. Karen had been given some dresses by the old Principessa which came down to her ankles and must have been made at the turn of the century. She looked like Ginger Rogers would have looked if Ginger Rogers had played Scarlett O'Hara.

Now that I didn't have to cable any more, I could spend my time with Bartlett. Our headquarters was a table in front of Vincent's café. Bartlett got up around ten in the morning and wandered down to Vincent's, where we sat until lunchtime. In the afternoon we napped and then went back to the café. He was still sweating out his call to Tommy and occasionally he went over to the post office to see if there was any news.

Karen had met the village priest, who spoke a little

English. She decided to learn Italian so they made an agreement. In exchange for his teaching her Italian, Karen promised to teach the priest English.

When I heard about it, I offered to teach Karen Italian, but Bartlett heard me make the offer and said it was better for her to learn from the priest.

If I hadn't known Bartlett I would have thought he was getting jealous.

Montecatini hung around for a few days and then decided to leave. He said he had investigated the theft of our trunks and he had some suspects in mind.

"You don't need any suspects," Bartlett told him at Vincent's café the morning Montecatini announced he was going. "Mondello stole our trunks."

"A good policeman never jumps to conclusions," Montecatini lectured. "All we know is that Mondello robbed you. But it is perfectly possible other bandits robbed your friend. After all, he admits it was at night and he didn't see their faces."

Bartlett said, "Inspector, do you think we'll ever see our stuff again?"

"Perhaps," suggested Montecatini, "you could offer a reward."

"You're a big help."

"Oh, there is one more thing," the Inspector said. "According to Italian law you must report to the carabiniere twice a week. The carabiniere in this district is Pasquale over there. Hey, Pasquale."

Pasquale, a thin, sad-faced policeman, wearing a dusty and bleached uniform, ambled over. Montecatini introduced us. Then he got into the Buick, waved to us and rode off.

When his car had disappeared, Pasquale looked furtively around and then said, "Signor Bartelini, may I talk to you frankly?"

Bartlett said he could.

"The Inspector said you should report to me twice a week, but you are a big man and I am a little man and so I will report to you twice a week."

"That's very generous of you, Pasquale."

"In return, Signor Bartelini, I need your help."

"I imagined as much," Bartlett said.

"The authorities in Palermo have no understanding of the problems here in La Coma. Last year, it will be exactly a year tomorrow, someone stole my bicycle. I reported it to Palermo and they refused to replace the bicycle. They said if I was a good policeman, I would find the thief *and* my bicycle. But how can I find the thief if I have no bicycle to look for him?

"Perhaps," said Pasquale, "you know someone in Rome, a high authority in the police department, and if you told him my problem he would order Palermo to give me another bicycle?"

"I'll go one further than that," Bartlett said. "I'll buy you a new bicycle."

Gratitude gleamed in Pasquale's eyes. He kissed Bartlett's hand. "Oh, Signor Bartelini, how can I thank you? I know, from now on, I'll report to you *every* day."

William stayed close to Bartlett when he was in town. He had bought an army .45 from one of the men in the village and he wore it in such a way that it deterred the Frasconis from starting any immediate trouble.

We held court at Vincent's every day. The Mayor was very interested in the loan Bartlett had mentioned in his speech and he was wondering how long it would take to get it.

Bartlett told him it was just a matter of months before he saw an influential friend of the Secretary of State and discussed La Coma with him.

"But," the Mayor said, "the Secretary of State would never be interested in what happens in La Coma."

"The Secretary of State is interested in the same things I am interested in."

The Mayor went away impressed.

Another time, the priest stopped by to see Bartlett. He wanted to know if Bartlett could possibly make the American Army pay for his church steeple. It seemed the Americans had hit the steeple with a bomb, and they promised to pay for it, but the priest had never heard from them again.

Bartlett said he would check with his connections in the Pentagon.

Many of the townspeople had business propositions for Bartlett. One wanted him to build a Cassata ice cream factory in La Coma. Another wanted him to buy a ranch and raise cattle. A third thought the thing La Coma really needed was a winery.

Bartlett, who had nothing better to do with his time, heard everyone out.

I didn't mind sitting in front of Vincent's. The sun felt

fine and, besides, I was getting good material for the series. I tried to be alone with Karen a few times but either William or Bartlett always popped up.

She wasn't digging La Coma and she felt her chances for a movie career were fading away.

At the end of the week, when Bartlett still didn't get his call through, he decided to go into Palermo.

He asked Pasquale to get him a car.

"But," said Pasquale, "you can't go to Palermo. You must not leave La Coma."

"Who says so?"

"The police."

"You're the police."

"I'm only one policeman," Pasquale said. "The other police in Palermo and Rome, they are the ones who say it."

"What would they do if I went to Palermo?"

"They could send you to Ustica, Signor Bartelini."

"Where's Ustica?"

"It's an island off Palermo where they send people to punish them. You have to stay there from one to five years, depending on how long the authorities want to keep you. They call it *confino*."

"But I haven't committed a crime."

"You don't have to. That's where they send people who haven't committed crimes."

"How can they send away people who haven't committed a crime?"

"I don't know," admitted Pasquale, "but they do it all the time."

"Isn't there any appeal?"

"The Supreme Court ruled it was unconstitutional, but it doesn't matter."

"Tell me something. Why is it that everything the Supreme Court rules unconstitutional, they still do in Italy?"

"It's democracy, Signor Bartlett. Under the Fascist government, people could do nothing. Now they can do everything."

After Pasquale left, Bartlett said, "I think I'll send William into Palermo to call New York and buy us a car."

"Ask him to get me a typewriter. And he also might get Karen some clothes. Can I get personal, Frank?"

"You're always getting personal," Bartlett said.

"Why don't you let Karen go to Rome?"

"I'm not stopping her."

"Yeah, but your mob in New York has her scared silly. They claim they're going to attach a time bomb to her mother. I think I know you pretty well now, and you don't seem like a guy who would hold a dame against her will."

Bartlett looked over at me. "Frankly, I've been tempted to let her go," he said, "but I just don't have the nerve. As long as she's here with me, I figure I have a chance of getting out of this dump. If she goes, I'll lose my mind."

"That's not rational," I protested. "She has nothing to do with your situation. Why do you want her around?"

"Sometimes, Pete," Bartlett said, getting up, "you're a pretty dumb guy."

Karen was starting to talk pretty good Italian by the

end of the week. She insisted we converse in Italian with her, all except William, who said he was happier not understanding the language. The glow of Bartlett's return had worn off for everyone including the townspeople after the first seven days.

On Sunday afternoon, I was sitting with Bartlett and William in front of Vincent's. We were surrounded by fishermen dressed in their Sunday best.

"Is it true," a fisherman asked, "that America is as we see it in the movies?"

"Yes," said Bartlett, "it is true."

"How big is America?" a fisherman asked.

"It's very big. Bigger than Italy and Capri put together."

"Do the fishermen own their own boats?"

"Not only their own boats, but their own cars. One car, sometimes two."

The fishermen snickered in disbelief.

"No fisherman could own a car," one of them said.

"How much does a fisherman make in the United States?"

Bartlett said, "Between 200,000 and 500,000 lire a month."

"He's full of wind," one of them said.

The tall fisherman who had danced with me, and whose name I had discovered was Pietro, got up. "If Mr. Bartelini says it's so, then it's so."

"You're a liar," one of the men said.

Pietro pulled the man up from his chair and socked him. One of the other fishermen picked up a beer bottle and crashed it across Pietro's head. He staggered. Another fisherman was going to hit Bartlett but William grabbed him around the head. A third fisherman picked up a chair and swung it at William. The table was knocked over and Bartlett was against the wall. He swung out at somebody coming at him. I tried to duck out of the melée but I didn't make it. A wine bottle caught me just above the ear. I went down, and it seemed the best place to stay. I heard the wives screaming and saw them, from my prone position, running toward the café. Vincent was cursing and swinging at everybody. Then the priest, his black gown flapping, came running across the square. He shouted at them to stop the fighting. Slowly, the violence abated.

"You should be ashamed of yourselves, fighting on Sundays."

He yelled at all of them. When he had finished, the wives started screaming at their husbands, pointing to the torn Sunday clothes. When I was sure it was safe, I got to my feet. Bartlett was nursing a bruised jaw, William a sprained shoulder and I a big headache.

Vincent was trying to put the pieces of his café together. He told Bartlett he couldn't sit there any more.

Bartlett gave him a 10,000-lire note and Vincent immediately set up a table and chairs for us.

We ordered a bottle of wine.

"That was the most fun I've had since I got to Italy," William said.

Bartlett said, "I enjoyed it too. At least, it made me feel like a man again."

"That priest would have to stop it," I said.

"You looked pretty, laid out there," Bartlett said to me.

"I was afraid the *News-Press* had lost its star crime reporter."

"I was biting their ankles," I said.

While we were sitting there reliving the battle, an old empty truck drove into the square. The driver jumped out of the cab and walked over.

He had on a sports shirt and a loud striped suit. I noticed a knife scar across his left cheek.

As he came closer, William made a move for his gun.

"Hiya, Frankie," the man said. "You remember me? Smokey Donetti of Chicago?"

Bartlett pretended he wasn't there.

"Beat it," William said.

"Wait a minute, Frankie. Hear me out. I'm no longer with Rizzolli's gang. I'm a deportee just like you."

"Hoods like you should have been deported a long time ago," Bartlett said. "Now beat it."

"I didn't come here for social talk," Smokey said. "I've come to offer you a business proposition. All the guys in Naples—the deportees—are real glad you're here, Frankie, honest we are. When we read in the paper that Frank Bartlett was one of us, we said, 'Maybe things will look up for us now.' The boys chipped in, every cent they had, and told me to go see you. Things are real bad in Naples, Frankie."

"What's that got to do with me?"

"You don't understand, Frankie. Naples is worse than any jail in America. Our lives are living hells. We can't get jobs and we can't get into rackets. The Neapolitans treat us like we was lepers or something. Some of us even

*111*

tried to do honest work, but we couldn't get any. People in Naples are worse than American cops."

"I'm not interested in your hard-luck stories."

Smokey, ignoring Bartlett's remark, continued, "Once in a while, the American fleet comes in and we can earn a few bucks showing the sailors around and getting them girls. But it ain't very patriotic, even if penicillin is available."

"I'm crying for you," Bartlett said.

"You don't understand the situation, Frankie. The Italians don't give a damn whether we live or die.

"We was going to march on Rome and make an official protest to the American Embassy, but they wouldn't let us leave Naples. Besides, each time we turn around, they steal us blind. Most of us would rather be doing time in the States than living free in Naples.

"You remember Harry the Hipster from Denver? He heard a bunch of wops knocking the United States in a bar and he took a swing at them. He got nine months. Nine months for defending the United States of America. Can you believe that?"

"You're boring me," Bartlett said.

"But that isn't what I came here to talk to you about. The boys thought, seeing as you were one of us now, that you've got an ideal situation for a business proposition. As you know, cigarettes are still one of the big items in this country. Now if we could use the fishing boats here to smuggle in the cigarettes from Tangiers, we could make a million dollars. No one has this territory down here. It's wide open."

"I'm not interested," Bartlett said.

"Frankie, all we need is financing and leadership. This is right up your alley. You keep fifty per cent, we keep fifty per cent. It's a real good thing."

Bartlett stood up. William stood behind Smokey. "Now, listen to me, you punk. I'm not interested in your proposition or the Naples boys. I'm getting out of here in a couple of weeks and I'm keeping my hands clean. The law says I ain't supposed to associate with crumbs like you, so get the hell out before I throw you out."

Smokey said, "Okay, big man. I'll give the boys your message. But you have no right to talk to me like that. In our eyes, you're just another stinking deportee."

William said, "Can I let him have it?"

Bartlett said, "Let Pasquale handle it."

Pasquale, who was standing by the doorway, came over and demanded to see Smokey's papers.

"Okay, Frankie," Smokey said. "You win. But maybe you could give me a few bucks to take care of my expenses."

Bartlett took a fifty-dollar bill out of his pocket. "Don't come back."

Smokey scooped up the money and said, "Thanks."

Pasquale escorted him to the truck.

William said, "You shouldn't have given him nothing, boss."

All the good humor from the fight had drained out of Bartlett. "If I don't get out of here soon, I'm going to blow my top," he said.

I decided, from the series point of view, it was worth while for me to stick around.

## 12

THE next morning at the café, Bartlett told William he would have to go to Palermo. "I'll never get a telephone call through to Stanton. I'll write down what I want you to tell him. Also, pick up a small car for around a thousand bucks and get Pasquale a bike."

"I'll go," said William. "But what about the Frasconi brothers? They're liable to start trouble."

"I think I know how to handle them." Bartlett turned to Pasquale. "Tell the Frasconi brothers I want to see them."

Pasquale didn't have far to go. The brothers were hanging out down the street. Pasquale brought them to the café.

Bartlett told them to sit down. They both eyed him suspiciously but finally took chairs. Bartlett ordered a bottle of wine. The brothers refused to taste it until we drank the wine first. As soon as they saw it wasn't poisoned, they helped themselves. I discovered the older brother's name was Giulio, the younger, Emmanuele.

"I want to call off the vendetta," Bartlett said.

"You can't," Giulio replied.

"Why not?" Bartlett asked.

"Because you didn't start it. It was started by our grandfathers."

"What is the solution?"

"One of our families has to be wiped out."

"Isn't there any other solution?"

Both brothers shook their heads.

"What was the cause of the vendetta in the first place?" Bartlett asked.

"We don't know."

"Suppose," said Bartlett, "it started because my grandfather killed your grandfather's sheep.

"Our grandfather never had any sheep. He was a fisherman."

"Okay, suppose my grandfather wrecked your gandfather's boat."

"That could have happened," one of the brothers replied.

"Now, let us suppose after my grandfather wrecked your grandfather's boat, he offered to pay for it, even to buy a bigger and better boat."

"Your grandfather was a bastard. He would never do that."

"I'm just supposing he would," Bartlett said. "If he was willing to buy your grandfather another boat, then there wouldn't have been a vendetta."

"So what?"

"You both are fishermen, aren't you?"

"Yes."

"If I bought you another boat, a better one than you have now, would you be willing to call off the vendetta?"

"Why would you want to buy us a boat?"

"Because," Bartlett said, "my grandfather wrecked your grandfather's boat."

The brothers chewed this one over in their slow minds.

"He's right, Giulio," one of the brothers said. "Besides, we could use a new boat."

"Would you be willing to call off the vendetta?"

"Our families would be very angry if we called off the vendetta," Giulio said.

"But you would have a new boat."

"A new boat is better than a vendetta," Emmanuele agreed.

"Particularly," I pointed out, "during the fishing season."

"We will need a few days to think it over," the brothers said.

"Is there a truce while you're thinking it over?"

The two brothers conferred. "Are we still pigs?" Emmanuele asked.

"Not while the truce is on," Bartlett said.

We all drank to the truce and the Frasconi brothers got up to go.

"We'll let you know about the boat."

"Boss," said William after they left, "you're a genius."

Just as we were finishing lunch at the castle that afternoon, Alfredo came into the dining room and whispered something in the Principessa's ear. She dropped her napkin and jumped up.

"The tuna are running today!" she cried. "Come and see it."

The old woman, still dressed in her black dress, put on a black hat and grabbed a heavy pair of work gloves. She took us around to the stable at the side of the castle. Her son was following us, but she yelled at him, "You can walk."

He turned around obediently and started down the hill.

The butler had put on a black chauffeur's cap, and he was trying to back a 1934 Lancia out of the garage.

"Hurry up, you fool," the Principessa screamed. "They're probably cheating me already."

"Who's cheating you?" I asked.

"Those worthless fishermen. The tuna belongs to me— all of it. If I'm not here they will sneak one away. I know the thieving fishermen of La Coma."

Alfredo managed to get the car turned around and the Principessa, Karen, Bartlett and I jumped in. But the engine of the Lancia died just as we all got comfortable.

The Principessa shouted at Alfredo to start.

I looked at the gas gauge. The gauge said the tank was empty.

"Your gas tank is empty," I said.

"Is that true?" the Principessa yelled at Alfredo.

"Sì," said Alfredo.

"What happened to the gasoline?" the Principessa shrilled. "I had a full tank."

"That was a month ago," Alfredo said.

"There should be some left. You've been using the car without my permission."

"No, Principessa," Alfred cried.

"I'll attend to you later," the Principessa said. "Come on, we'll push it down the road. We can coast to the docks."

Bartlett and Alfredo and the old Principessa and I got out and pushed the old Lancia down the hill.

When we got to the road, we all jumped into the car and rolled down the mountainside with Alfredo trying to control the steering wheel while, at the same time, keeping his hand on the horn. Children, chickens and townspeople, recognizing the Principessa's horn, all jumped out of the road just in time.

The car barreled down the narrow streets, almost knocking over a donkey. Karen and Bartlett had their hands over their eyes. At last we screamed into the port and Alfredo pumped the brakes. The Lancia stopped just before it went into the water.

The old lady jumped out of the car and, waving a large key in her hand, rushed to the weighing shed. The first boats were already bringing in the tuna.

The rest of us, shaken by the ride, got out of the Lancia slowly.

Pietro, our friend of the fight, was on the dock. He tried to enter the shed, but the Principessa pushed him out. "You stay here, Pietro. You know you're not allowed in the weighing shed."

Pietro spat and walked over to where we were standing.

"The old bitch," he said.

"What's going on?" Bartlett asked.

"No one but she and her idiot son are allowed in the

weighing shed. We get paid by percentage, thirty per cent of the catch. But she's the only one who is allowed to look at the scales."

Karen said to Bartlett, "Ask him if they catch all of the tuna by hand."

Bartlett translated the question.

"No," said Pietro. "It's done by nets. Every year the tuna come along the coast and lay their eggs. The nets run out to that buoy there. The tuna follow the nets and suddenly they find themselves in what we call the death chamber. We wait until as many tuna are in the death chamber as possible and then we pull in the nets and kill them by knocking them over the head."

When Bartlett translated the answer, Karen laughed and said, "It sounds like one of your operations."

Before he could reply, the Principessa came storming out of the shed. "Someone has stolen the bulb from the socket!"

Pietro went meekly over to the shed. "But, Principessa, the shed was locked."

"Then someone must have a key. Find Pasquale and have the thief arrested. I can't be buying new light bulbs all the time."

She went back into the shed.

As the men unloaded the tuna, they were singing a song.

"What are they singing?" Karen asked.

I asked Pietro.

"It's an old Sicilian song. The sad story of two tuna fish. One sunny day, the fishermen capture a female tuna and

*119*

drag her ashore. But they see another tuna coming toward them. As the fishermen pull in the female, the other tuna, a male, leaps out of the sea to join the dying female. He could not live without her and prefers to die on the beach next to her rather than swim in the sea alone."

"It's the story of boy tuna and girl tuna," I told Karen. "Boy tuna meets girl tuna, falls in love, before they can marry girl tuna is captured by fishermen. The lovers separate. In the end, boy tuna crawls up on beach to die next to girl tuna, rather than be the only fish in the sea."

"It's more beautiful the way they sing it, Pete," Karen said.

Pietro said, "It's the first catch of the season, and the men are very happy. There will be food on the tables tonight."

"You mean to say," Bartlett said, "you only get paid when you bring in tuna?"

Pietro nodded.

"But what if there are no tuna?"

"Then we have nothing. We must borrow from the Principessa on our future earnings and we are all in debt to her."

"Why don't you have a union?"

Pietro spat again. "She would destroy us if we mentioned the word union. She would take our boats and even our houses. The del Grandis have been operating like this for centuries.

We watched the fishermen unload the tuna and drag it onto the scales. Every time a tuna was placed on the scales, the Principessa would yell out from the shed and a groan would go up from the fishermen, who were sure the tuna weighed thirty kilos more than she said.

Once Pietro was so enraged he charged the shed and shouted that the Principessa was cheating them.

"You whoremonger's son," the Principessa yelled. "They're my scales and I'll weigh them as I like."

The weighing went on for hours. Karen had an appointment for an Italian lesson and she left us, but Bartlett and I stood watching the operation with interest.

A hunchbacked man was standing near us. I didn't pay any attention to him until he wandered casually over and greeted us.

We nodded. He looked different from other La Coma men in that he was dressed in city clothes, including a Panama straw hat.

"It is interesting work," he said, starting up a conversation.

"Dangerous, too," he continued.

We both looked at him curiously. He gave us a toothless grin.

"But then again, everything we do is dangerous."

"You're the town philosopher," I said.

"Mr. Bartelini looks very healthy since he came to La Coma."

"The air has done me a lot of good," Bartlett said sarcastically.

"La Coma," the hunchback said, "can be either the healthiest or the unhealthiest place in the world."

The hunchback turned his attention to the tuna. A few

minutes later he said, "This may sound strange, but what a man needs in La Coma more than anything else is protection."

Bartlett said, "What are you looking for, a job as a bodyguard?"

"No," replied the hunchback, taking out a cigarette. "I'm too old to work at such things. At one time, though, I was a very good bodyguard. Now I'm a collector."

"What do you collect?" Bartlett asked.

"Mr. Bartelini, I represent an organization that is interested in protecting the interests of the people of Sicily. Would you want to buy our service?"

Bartlett started laughing. "The shakedown racket," he said to me. Then to the hunchback, "I've got a bodyguard. Thanks just the same."

"But," protested the hunchback, "our organization gives you far better protection than a bodyguard could give you. We have people all over. They see to it that no rocks fall on your head. They make sure when you're down here at the port no one pushes you into the sea. And we can personally insure you a long and happy life in La Coma."

"Mister," said Bartlett, smiling, "I know more about the shakedown racket than you'll ever know. Go peddle your services someplace else. I'm not interested."

"It's very cheap," the hunchback persisted. "For 200,000 lire a week, you can have full coverage."

"No soap. I'll take my chances on rocks falling on my head. But you better tell your people William is armed and if anything starts up there's going to be a lot of shooting around La Coma."

"I beg you, for the sake of your father whom I knew so well, to reconsider. You are a rich man, and 200,000 lire is nothing to you."

Bartlett said, "How many times do I have to tell you I'm not interested?"

The hunchback shook his head sadly and walked away.

Pietro, who had been helping unload the tuna fish, came over to us. "I see Antonio has been trying to sell you an insurance policy."

"I didn't buy any," Bartlett said. "I don't need protection from an old crippled man. Who is he, anyway?"

"Antonio is a collector for the Mafia."

"The Mafia? I thought that was a gag."

"It is no gag, Signor Bartelini. The Mafia are the real rulers of Sicily. When one rules, one must collect taxes. That is what Antonio does. He collects taxes."

"Does everyone in La Coma pay the Mafia?"

"Only those who can afford it. Even the Principessa must pay. Once she didn't and the Mafia threw a freshly killed lamb into her tuna nets. The sharks smelled the blood and the tuna nets were ruined. The Principessa paid after that. Of course, she makes it up by cheating on her Italian taxes. To her, it adds up to the same thing."

"I don't go for shakedowns," Bartlett said. "I never paid a dime in my life for protection. If they want to start something I'm ready for them."

"Please don't think I'm interfering," Pietro said. "But you should take the Mafia more seriously. You have no other protection here."

123

"I've got my bodyguard, and if worst comes to worst, I've got Pasquale."

Pietro laughed. "Pasquale, that's a good one. One day Pasquale ordered one of the Mafia to put on his shirt in the square. The Mafia man became so angry he took Pasquale's bike and has been riding around on it ever since. Pasquale pretends it has been stolen, but everyone in town knows where the bicycle is, including Pasquale."

"Anyway," said Bartlett, "I'm not going to be here that long."

Pietro said, "But you just got here. Don't you like La Coma?"

"Sure," said Bartlett, "I love it."

At dinner that evening, the Principessa and her son were still down at the docks and Bartlett, Karen and I dined alone.

"What do you do with yourself all day?" I asked.

"I walk," said Karen angrily. "It's good for the legs, especially if I want to go into the tuna-fish business."

"You're certainly carrying a chip on your shoulder."

"Chip on my shoulder? I've been kidnaped, my clothes have been stolen, I'm dressed up as an extra for *Wuthering Heights* and I don't have a ticket back to the United States. I'll say I'm carrying a chip on my shoulder."

I looked over at Bartlett to see his reaction. He said, "Perhaps I shouldn't have let William talk me into letting you come. Okay, so I made a mistake. I'll make a deal with you. Anytime you want to leave, I'll give you the dough."

"Are you serious?" Karen asked.

"Dead serious," Bartlett replied. "Maybe when I get back to the States, we can have dinner together and talk about our La Coma days."

"That's a good idea. Sort of a reunion," I said.

"I didn't invite you," Bartlett said.

"What's getting into him?" Karen asked me.

"Maybe it's the glow of La Coma," I suggested. "It does different things to different people."

"I'm being kind to blondes this week," Bartlett said. "Besides, it wasn't your idea to come on this joy ride."

Karen said, "This is the last thing I expected. What about your kind friends who insist on everyone honoring contracts?"

"Don't worry about them."

"And William?"

"William won't bother you. When do you want to go?"

"I . . . I don't know. I can't leave until I have some clothes."

"I told William to bring you back some."

"Hey," said Karen all of a sudden, "are you trying to get rid of me?"

Bartlett laughed. "Nobody believes my intentions any more. I think I'll become a priest." He left the table.

Karen looked over at me. "Now I'm really confused."

"Go, while the going's good."

"Now you're trying to get rid of me."

"Heck, no," I said. "But I can always catch up with you someplace else. Bartlett can't. I think you're falling for Bartlett. Stranger things have happened in La Coma."

"You must be crazy," and she dashed out of the room.

125

I found myself eating my cheese alone. I also found myself hoping the assignment would be over soon. The only thing I didn't know, and would have to hang around to find out, was whether Bartlett was going to remain in La Coma for a while. If he was, the story would have a much more interesting ending.

# 13

Two days later, William came back from Palermo, driving a Fiat. On top was Pasquale's bicycle. Bartlett and I rushed out to meet him on the castle steps. He told us it was a stolen car but the police would never be able to trace it. "It only cost half of what a regular-priced Fiat would cost," he said proudly.

"What are you fooling around with hot cars for?" Bartlett said angrily.

"I never bought a car on the open market," William said defensively, "and I'm not going to start now."

Bartlett was more interested in what Tommy had to say.

"It took me thirty-six hours to get through," William said. "When I finally did, the news wasn't so good. Tommy said Rizzolli has been telling the boys you're washed up. Lover-boy's stories about us getting held up by Mondello didn't do us any good either. The mob is the laughingstock of the East Coast."

Bartlett turned on me, his face darkening. "I thought you were my friend. Okay, buster, I don't need you around.

You can go any time you want to."

"I just wrote what happened," I protested. "You can see copies of my stories if you don't believe me."

"Any way you look at it," William said, "the organization is falling apart. Rizzolli has made an offer. He'll give you 500,000 bucks over a five-year period for the organization as it is."

"Screw him," Bartlett said. "I'll get him after my appeal."

"There is no appeal," William said. "The Supreme Court adjourned without hearing your case."

Bartlett cursed.

"Stanton," William said, "thinks you should have gone to the pen. He says it's easier to get an appeal when you're in the pen than when you're out of the country."

"That's just great," Bartlett said. "Now he tells me. What about me going to the pen now? At least I could watch things closer from there than from this dustbin."

"It's too late. Stanton says they won't let you back even to go to jail."

"What's the solution?"

William hesitated and then said, "Tommy said he thinks you should accept Rizzolli's offer."

"I'm not selling out to Rizzolli," Bartlett yelled. "It's my organization. I built it up from nothing. A lot of guys got hurt before it was whipped into shape. The organization may be going chicken on me but I'm not going chicken. I'll figure out a way of getting out of this hole, and when I do, I'll buy out Rizzolli, but not with dollars. What else did those finks have to say?"

"They wanted to know how you were getting along with the broad."

"That's dandy. What did you tell them?"

"I said you and she were hitting it off just great. I said she was the greatest lay you ever had."

Bartlett grabbed William by his shirt. "Don't you ever let me hear you say that again!"

"I'm sorry," William said. "I didn't know what to tell them."

"Did you bring my typewriter?" I asked William.

"Yeah. You owe me eighty-nine dollars. It's a new Olivetti."

"Stolen?"

William grinned. "The stores were all out of them."

Bartlett said, "You can go do your typing somewhere else. I'm not talking to you any more. I don't like guys that double-cross me."

"If only you could understand, Frank. I wrote it the way it happened. I didn't add one thing."

"Well, apparently you shouldn't have written it the way it happened. You heard what William said. I'm the laughingstock of the United States. I should have learned my lesson years ago. Never be friends with a newspaperman."

"Okay, Frank," I said. "I'll clear out if that's the way you want it. But your friends are getting few and far between. You're going to need them soon."

"I don't need anybody," Bartlett said. "Especially a lying rat like you."

I took off the watch and tossed it to him, and walked into the castle.

I met Karen as I went down to my room.

"I'm conjugating 'to kidnap' in Italian," she said.

"That's fine."

"What's your problem?"

"I'm leaving this burg."

"When?"

"Tomorrow."

"You're not going to leave me here!"

"I thought you liked it here."

"I'm not going to stay here without you," Karen said. "I don't like it that much. What's the rush?"

"Bartlett doesn't believe in freedom of the press. He told me to scram."

"He can't tell you to scram against your will."

"I need his co-operation. Don't you understand, Karen? I can stay in La Coma, but it would just be a waste of time if he wouldn't talk to me. I guess I have enough for a series anyway. Do you want to come with me?"

"I don't have any clothes."

"William brought you some from Palermo."

"I might as well. Maybe I'll go to Rome after all."

"You don't sound very excited about leaving," I said.

"La Coma grows on you," she said.

"The bus stops down the road at nine tomorrow morning. If you want to come, be ready."

I went to my room to gather together my few possessions.

At dinnertime, the Principessa said to me, "You used two towels this week."

"I'm sorry. I must have lost my head," I said. "I'm leaving tomorrow, so give me all my bills."

"Oh," said the Principessa. "Where are you going?"

"Probably back to the United States."

Karen looked over at Bartlett. "I'm leaving also."

Bartlett went white.

"You can't leave," William said roughly.

"Shut up, William," Bartlett said. Then to Karen he said, "That's a pretty sudden decision."

Karen said, "It's been on my mind for some time. I was just waiting for some clothes."

"You two are heading off together, huh?" Bartlett asked.

"We're taking the same bus, if that's what you mean," I said.

Bartlett's hand was shaking. I almost felt sorry for him at that moment. "Well, it's been a lot of fun," he finally said.

Karen said, "I must say it's been an experience."

"I'm not sure," said the Principessa, "I can keep Mr. Bartelini and his friend much longer. I said it would be a temporary thing only."

As soon as dinner was over I wandered into the library to write some letters. I overheard William and Bartlett arguing in the hall. "She has a lot of nerve," William said. "I'm going to tell her where to get off."

"We can't keep her here against her will. Don't try to stop her, William, and if you tell the boys what happened, I'll never forgive you."

"I never saw things in such a mess," William said.

"Just keep the gas tank filled," Bartlett said. "We're not going to be around here much longer ourselves."

William replied, "Now you're talking, boss."

The next morning at eight o'clock, I met Karen downstairs. She was dressed in her suit and was carrying a small valise.

"You want to say good-by to Bartlett?" I asked her.

"I said good-by to him last night."

"Oh?" I said.

"I don't care what anybody says. I'm going to Rome and I'm going to be an actress!"

"Don't yell at me. I didn't say you weren't. Do you have enough dough?"

"Yes," she said. "And I'll send him back every nickel."

"The way things are going for him, he might need it."

We made our farewells to the Principessa.

"Are you sure you don't want to marry my son?" she asked.

"I'm very sure," Karen replied.

"There's nothing wrong with him, is there?"

"It's not that. I want to have a career. I want to be a movie actress."

"Movies, bah!" the Principessa scowled. "All the girls want to get into the movies these days. None of them are interested in tuna fishing."

"Maybe with television," I said, "they'll get interested in tuna fishing again."

We shook hands and I picked up Karen's bag and my portable and walked down to the bus stop. Neither of us looked back.

The bus was fifteen minutes late. We found two seats in the back, and as the bus pulled out I noticed Karen wiping her eyes.

I didn't say anything, but a half hour later I said, "You

did fall for Bartlett, didn't you?"

She sniffled and nodded her head.

"Why? How? How can a dame fall for a guy like that?"

Karen said, her eyes filling again, "Chemistry. Everything went poof."

"You're lucky you left," I said.

Karen said, "I'm not so sure."

I tried to make a case for myself. "Karen, I don't understand you. Here I am, a hard-working, honest, nose-to-the-grindstone reporter. I'm not bad looking, though I admit I'm not Rock Hudson. I'm not loaded with dough but I can support a wife. I'm kind and good to children, and I support my old mother. As a matter of fact, I'm everything a girl could hope for in a husband. How can you fall for a low-down bum like Bartlett?"

Karen blew her nose. "I told you, Pete. Chemistry."

"Horse manure," I said.

"There's more to it than that," Karen replied.

We arrived in Palermo in the afternoon. I decided to go up to Rome, not because Karen was going there, but because it was the best place to get a plane to the United States.

We decided to take the night ferry, which left at seven in the evening and arrived in Naples at six the next morning. I rented a horse and carriage and we went sightseeing. But Karen wasn't interested in the scenery. I was glad when it was almost time to leave. We arrived at the boat dock at six-thirty and were just about to board when a man came up and asked in English if she was Karen Withers. She said she was and he asked if he could speak to her. I said I was a friend of the family and the three of us went over to a café.

The man said, "I have information that your friend Mr. Bartelini and his friend have been kidnaped, and I have been told to contact you."

"If this is a gag on his part, it isn't going to work. I told him I'm not going to stay and I meant it," Karen said.

"It is not a joke," the man said. "I speak the truth. Last night your friends were taken by persons unknown to parts unknown and are being held for ransom. I understand the sum is one hundred thousand dollars."

"A hundred thousand dollars? What do you expect me to do about it?" Karen said.

"I suppose you are to pay the ransom."

"I don't have *one* thousand, much less a hundred thousand."

"But you are his woman. You know where to get the money."

"I don't know where to get the money," protested Karen. "What will happen if the money is not produced?"

The man shook his head sadly. "They will have to kill them."

"Does Mondello have anything to do with this?" I asked.

He looked me straight in the eye. "Who is Mondello?"

Karen said, "I haven't got any money."

"You can get it from his friends. We understand that Mr. Bartelini is a very influential man in the United States. His friends would be happy to pay the slight sum of one hundred thousand dollars for his safe return."

"Will you take four hundred and fifty dollars?" Karen asked.

The man laughed. "One hundred thousand dollars. We understand Mr. Bartelini brought over seventy thousand dollars with him so if you could find that you would not have to add much to it."

The boat whistle blew and the man got up to leave.

"Whom do I contact?" Karen asked.

"Go back to La Coma. We'll contact you."

The boat whistle blew again.

"Are you leaving?" I asked Karen.

"Aren't you?"

"Not on your life. This story may get me the Pulitzer Prize."

"Well, I'm not going to leave either. What should we do now?"

"I guess we'd better go back to La Coma."

I decided not to file the story, as it would only bring every reporter within two thousand miles to Sicily. I hoped to meet Mondello again and get an exclusive interview with him. I was much happier than Karen when we got back on the bus that evening to go to La Coma.

We got back after midnight. It took us some time before we could get Alfredo to open the door. He told us the Principessa was outraged because she thought Bartlett and William had skipped out on her without paying the sums due. I told Alfredo that Bartlett and William had been kidnaped and he said, "The Principessa will be very happy to hear about it."

Alfredo showed us back to our old rooms.

The next morning the Principessa greeted us coldly and had no kinds words to say about Bartlett. I promised her if Bartlett didn't come back, the *News-Press* would pay her bill. Lucas would have fainted away, but with this guarantee the Principessa said we could stay.

After breakfast, Karen and I walked down into town. We expected to be contacted right away and we took up a station at Vincent's café. But no one bothered us. It was apparent from the looks on people's faces that they knew about Bartlett's kidnaping, but they pretended nothing had happened.

I was going over in my mind the possibilities involved.

I wondered where Bartlett did put the seventy thousand dollars. The people who kidnaped him must have known about it. Mondello, on the very first day, must have known about it. Perhaps that is why he was so disinterested in the few hundred dollars he found in Bartlett's wallet. I remembered Montecatini's words, "You will discover nothing is a secret and everything is a secret in Sicily."

Even Pasquale knew and indicated as much to me at Vincent's.

"It is very sad," Pasquale said. "Mr. Bartelini was a very nice man."

"Have you reported the kidnaping to Palermo?" I asked.

"Oh, no," said Pasquale. "After losing my bicycle and then having this happen right under my nose, I would only be reprimanded."

"So you're not going to do anything?" I asked hopefully.

"What is there to do? Either Mr. Bartelini will be returned to La Coma or he will be killed. If he is killed, I shall have to report it, particularly since the other man is an American, but it's better to wait. These kidnapings go one way or the other very quickly."

"Do you have many of them?"

"All the time. It is not my place to suggest, but if Mr. Bartelini had paid the Mafia what they asked of him, this never would have happened."

I was happy Pasquale was not going to inform the authorities.

Nothing happened that day, but the next day the hunchback sent us a note to meet him at the port. He had a package under his arm, which he gave to Karen.

"What is it?" Karen asked.

"Open and see," the hunchback replied.

We tore open the package and recognized Bartlett's and William's khaki pants. There were bloodstains smeared on them.

"You murdered him!" Karen cried.

"Not yet," the hunchback said. "But we don't want to wait too long. Give us the seventy thousand dollars and we will free him."

"I don't know anything about the seventy thousand dollars," Karen said.

"She doesn't," I told the hunchback. "If it exists, only Bartlett knows where it is. We don't have the slightest idea."

"He doesn't seem to want to tell us," the hunchback said. "He's a very stubborn man."

I gave the bloody pants back to the hunchback and took Karen to Vincent's.

"We should tell the police," Karen said.

"It would be very dangerous," I said. "If they got on the trail, Mondello might panic and kill both of them. We'll have to think of something else."

"Maybe we could cable Bartlett's friends and they could send the money?" Karen said.

"It's an outside chance. But we might try it."

I remembered Stanton's office was in the Chrysler Building and I cabled him: BARTLETT IN TROUBLE. NEEDS SEVENTY THOUSAND DOLLARS URGENTLY. PLEASE SEND CARE OF AMERICAN EXPRESS, and signed my name.

The following day, I received a reply: IMPOSSIBLE TO RAISE SEVENTY THOUSAND DOLLARS FOR BARTLETT. DOUBT IF I COULD RAISE SEVEN THOUSAND DOLLARS. REGRETS STANTON.

I showed the telegram to the hunchback and translated it for him. He wasn't happy at all.

"Now it's up to Bartelini," he said. "But he doesn't have much time."

Karen decided to write Bartlett a letter. She showed it to me and I almost got sick. It said, "Darling, please give the men what they ask for. I love you and I want you back alive. Love, Karen."

"Don't you think it's kind of sentimental?" I said.

"I meant every word I said."

All I could answer was, "Poof."

Two bloody shirts were delivered to us the next day. I figured if Bartlett and William got out of this alive, they would both need transfusions.

At last came a note from Bartlett. It said, "Darling, in my bedroom in the closet on the floor you will see three boards. Pry up the middle one and you will find the money belt. Please bring it to me. I love you too."

Karen kissed me, she was so happy. "Let's go," she said.

I asked the hunchback what we should do with the money once we had it.

"Give it to me," he said.

"Oh, no," I said. "We don't even know if Bartlett and William are still alive. We'll deliver it ourselves."

The hunchback sent us a message in the afternoon to be at a statue of the Madonna a mile outside of La Coma at midnight. There would be men and horses ready to escort us to Mondello's hideout.

# 14

KAREN and I went back to the castle and followed Bartlett's instructions. We found the money belt where he said it would be. I opened it and whistled. Karen looked and she whistled.

"I've never seen so much money."

"Well, take another look," I told her. "Because you may never see it again."

I told Karen not to wear her suit that evening. She put on one of the Principessa's dresses instead.

"Have you ever ridden a horse?" I asked her.

"Heck, no," Karen said.

"I never have either," I confessed.

We sneaked out of the castle an hour before midnight and hiked down the road to the statue.

We waited at the Madonna, and a little after one we heard horses coming out of the woods. There were two men and four horses. They insisted on blindfolding both

Karen and me before putting us on the horses. Then they warned us not to talk and mounted their own. Our horses were tied to them and we started the long ride toward Mondello's headquarters. The going was slow and Karen complained her seat hurt. But we never stopped. It must have taken us three hours to arrive at our destination.

Dawn was just coming up as we were helped off the horses and the blindfolds were taken off our eyes. We found ourselves high in a mountain clearing surrounded by bushes six feet high. There was a cave in the mountainside and off to the left was a small corrugated hut. A fire some twenty feet from the cave was blazing and about ten men were sitting around it drinking coffee.

Mondello came over to greet us.

"Where is he?" screamed Karen.

Mondello pointed to two freshly dug graves.

"You've killed him!"

Mondello shook his head.

Karen, crying, ran over to the graves. Bartlett, who was sleeping in one, woke up with a start.

"Darling," said Karen. "You're alive."

Bartlett tried to get out of the grave but Karen was kneeling in it and wouldn't let him get out.

"What are they doing in the graves?" I asked Mondello.

Mondello said, "I gave them the choice of sleeping in the tomb or the graves, so they said they preferred the graves. I didn't care. If you didn't bring the money, it would have saved me a lot of trouble."

Bartlett climbed out of the grave. I hardly recognized him. He had a week's growth of beard, his hair was matted and filthy, his clothes—what was left of them—were in tatters, and he was pretty shaky on his feet.

William, who climbed out of the other grave, seemed to have survived the ordeal a little better, though he also needed a shave and a strong Lysol bath.

When Karen saw Bartlett's condition, she screamed at Mondello, "You beasts, you monsters, you sadists."

"What is she saying?" Mondello asked.

"She says she brought the money."

"Good," Mondello said. "Let us count it."

Bartlett said, "Can we leave now?"

"Not until tonight," Mondello said. "It isn't safe to release you in the daytime."

I was delighted with the news as it would give me an opportunity to talk to Mondello. While he was counting the money and Karen was trying to put Bartlett back in shape, William told me what had happened.

Bartlett and he decided to leave the same night Karen and I announced our departure. They had parked the Fiat outside the castle gates so no one would hear them leave. Around midnight, they left and were driving toward Palermo when Bartlett remembered he had forgotten the money belt. William turned the car around and drove back. They parked the Fiat again outside the gate but as they got out of the car, four men came out of the dark and told them to put their hands up.

"I tried to make an escape but I got hit over the head. The last thing I remember was Bartlett struggling with two of the bastards.

"When I woke up I found myself slung over a mule like

a sack of flour. My hand and legs were tied. I could see the boss. He also was thrown over a mule. They were surely the oldest mules in Sicily because they kept slipping and falling down. To top things off, it started raining and every half mile we were both dumped in the mud.

"Once I yelled and Mondello whacked me with his leather strap. I could have killed him."

When they arrived at the camp, Mondello put William and Bartlett in the corrugated hut. There were a couple of straw mattresses in the hut and that was all. Mondello told them he was holding them for ransom, and if they didn't pay he'd kill them.

"The boss thought Mondello was bluffing but I wasn't so sure. In the beginning the meals weren't too bad, but as time went on they got worse and so did Mondello's temper. He made us dig an eight-foot pit over there and put us into it. He said the hut was too good for us. I kept telling the boss we had to pay, but he couldn't believe an Okie like Mondello could do this to him. The tomb was pretty hot, I'll tell you that.

"After that, when the boss wouldn't give in, Mondello made us dig those two graves. About this time even the boss decided things were getting desperate. So he sent the note to Karen."

Bartlett came over to where we were talking. He stuck out his hand. "I'm even glad to see you," he said.

I shook it. "Glad to see you, Frank. No hard feelings?"

"After this," said Bartlett, "I have no hard feelings toward anybody. Except him." He pointed to where Mondello was joyously counting the money.

"I'd give you your watch back," Bartlett said, "but he took it."

"That's all right," I said. "You can always get me another one."

Mondello finally finished counting the money. "It's all there; 73,198 dollars."

"I thought you said it was only 70,000 dollars."

"Ah," said Mondello, "the extra money is for food."

I told William what Mondello said. "Three grand for that food!" he exclaimed. "The guy ought to be arrested."

"Can I quote you?" I asked William.

Mondello served us all coffee and a plate of beans. I waited until he was seated before I wandered over to him.

"Have you heard from the President of the United States yet?" I asked him.

"No," he said dispiritedly. "But maybe he doesn't know where to reach me."

"It's possible. Of course if your letter was published in an American newspaper, the President would see it."

"That's a good idea," Mondello agreed.

I told him if he gave me a copy of the letter, I would see that it was printed.

Mondello went over to his saddle and took a piece of paper out of the pouch. "Here is a copy," he said.

It was in Italian.

DEAR PRESIDENT OF THE UNITED STATES:

On behalf of the people of Sicily, I wish to say we want to become the 49th state, as we are sick and tired of Italian administration and police. I promise you if you give your blessing I will see that every Sicilian is a good American or I will kill him. Please let me hear from you as soon as you can as I must keep moving. Write to the post office in La Coma. I can always get my letters that way.

GIUSEPPE MONDELLO

P.S. If you have an autographed picture of Rita Hayworth would you send it with your reply?

"That's a very good letter," I told Mondello. "And I don't understand why the President hasn't answered unless he's waiting for Rita Hayworth's photo."

"Maybe I should have put that in another letter," Mondello agreed.

Mondello said he was a great admirer of Rita Hayworth and George Raft. He never missed any American films.

"Can you go to the movies without the police seeing you?" I asked him.

"No," he said. "When a new picture plays in town, we wake the manager at two in the morning and he shows it to us all night. With Rita Hayworth I sometimes come back the next night to see her again.

"Once I kidnaped a Sicilian prince and he said he knew the husband of Rita Hayworth, a man named Khan. The prince promised me he would get her picture for me but the pig never did. The next time I see him, I'll cut the tongue out of his throat."

"If you keep on the way you're going," I said, "Rita Hayworth is going to be asking for your autograph."

This last remark seemed to please him very much.

I was curious to find out how Mondello became a bandit.

"Sicily is a poor place," he said, "with many poor people.

145

Everybody wants to keep you poor. I did not want to be poor and so I robbed, but only from people who I knew could afford it, like Bartelini over there. Then the Mafia asked me to kidnap people who would not pay them taxes. It wasn't hard work and it paid even better than robbery. But there are risks one takes with kidnaping. The men don't like it. It's too much sitting around."

I took notes on everything. In the afternoon I slept and by evening we were ready to leave.

Mondello made me promise to print his letter, a promise I assured him I would keep.

We were all blindfolded again and I must say there were no heartbreaking good-bys. Bartlett told Mondello, "If there is any justice in this world, you'll get yours."

Mondello, who was probably richer than he had ever been, laughed. "You, of all people, should know, Mr. Bartelini, money is justice, and I have it now."

It took us the best part of the night to get back to the statue of the Madonna. Then we were ordered off the horses and told to walk the rest of the way into town. Although it was early in the morning, we seemed to have awakened the whole town.

Pasquale came dashing out of his house buttoning his pants. He was visibly moved. "Mr. Bartelini, I am so happy to see you. I prayed to the Virgin for your safe return."

"Why didn't you try to find me?"

"And lose my new bicycle?"

Bartlett's aunt rushed up and kissed him. "We prayed for you, Francesco. Now our prayers are answered. At first we thought it was the Frasconi brothers, but when we saw them, they were as unhappy as we were. Tell me, did you really meet Mondello?"

"Yes, I did," Bartlett replied.

"You must tell us everything. Your cousins worship Mondello. He is their hero."

The hunchback was standing in the crowd that surrounded us. He smiled his toothless smile again. "Insurance would have been so much cheaper."

We started the long climb up to the castle. As soon as I got there, I rushed to my room and started typing my story.

It began, "La Coma, Sicily—America's best known racketeer, Frank Bartlett, was kidnaped this week in his home town of La Coma by Sicily's best known bandit, La Coma-born Giuseppe Mondello, and held for $100,000 ransom. Bartlett, who has been sitting in La Coma since he arrived in Italy because police officials wouldn't let him visit more glamorous places, was snatched with his bodyguard, William Condon of New York, and taken by horse to Mondello's headquarters high in the mountains that range around La Coma.

"Mondello apparently knew that Bartlett had brought American dollars with him, and insisted that Bartlett either turn the money over to him or face the consequences. The consequences were made clearer when Mondello forced Bartlett and Condon to dig their own graves. At this point, this reporter, who has been living in La Coma gathering material for a series on Bartlett, was instructed by Bartlett, through one of Mondello's men, to dig up 73,000 American dollars which Bartlett had hidden in the old castle of the Principessa del Grandi and deliver it to Mondello's man.

"This reporter found the money, but in order to make sure that Bartlett and Condon were still alive, he insisted on delivering it himself. On arrival at Mondello's hideout, we found Bartlett and Condon very much alive, but they had been through an ordeal.

"We turned the money over to Mondello and in exchange were given both men. Police authorities were not notified of the kidnaping for fear that Mondello might panic and do away with both men.

"In an exclusive interview with Mondello, this reporter learned that Bartlett had refused to pay protection money to the Mafia, Sicily's famed underground organization, and Mondello had been ordered to teach Bartlett an old Sicilian lesson. Mondello said he was delighted to make the acquaintance of America's leading racketeer and he was also happy to discover they had so much in common.

"This was not Mondello's first kidnaping. He has kidnaped many times before, but he said he kidnaps only adult male members of the family, and has never touched a woman or a child.

"At the present moment, he is awaiting a reply from the President of the United States in reference to an application he has made on behalf of the citizens of Sicily to become a forty-ninth state. Enclosed is a text of the letter."

The story ran three thousand words with a description of the hideaway, Mondello, his band of robbers, and the background on La Coma. I didn't mention Karen in the story; it would have been too difficult to explain what she was doing in La Coma, and besides, I didn't want to embarrass her. The truth is I didn't want to say she was in love with Bartlett.

Lucas cabled the next day and said it was the best story I had ever written.

Boyle cabled to say he had sold the series to eighty-five newspapers. My story was picked up and splashed across the front pages of the world. If it hadn't been for Karen, I would have felt like a million bucks.

Bartlett's cables weren't nearly as welcome as mine.

He wired Stanton for money and was turned down.

Then he sent another wire telling Stanton to accept Rizzolli's offer. The reply to this one, which the man in the post office showed me (he let me read everybody's cables and I'm sure he showed mine to everybody else), said: RIZZOLLI NO LONGER INTERESTED IN BUYING YOU OUT. IS TAKING OVER WITH BOYS' ASSENT. THEY FEEL YOU NOT COMING BACK AND AFRAID WITHOUT LEADERSHIP ORGANIZATION WILL CRUMBLE. SORRY FRANK BUT WE ALL HAVE TO FACE FACTS. REGARDS, STANTON.

I read the cable and decided it was the beginning of the end for one Frank Bartlett.

"What about your own money in America?" I asked Bartlett.

"I put it all in Stanton's name when the income-tax rap came up," he said. "I don't have a dime of my own. Stanton had better pay me if I don't come back, the . . ."

# 15

~~~~~~~~~~~~~~~~~~~~~~~~~~~~~~~

FRANCESCO BARTELINI, alias Frank Bartlett, was on the ropes. His friends in America had deserted him, he was without funds, except for the $800 he had given Karen, which she had returned to him, and his outlook for the future was far from bright. It was at this moment that help came from an unexpected source. Just when things were at their blackest, Smokey Donetti of Naples arrived back in La Coma.

I hardly recognized him when he drove up to Vincent's café. This time, Smokey was behind the wheel of a new Oldsmobile instead of a truck. He was dressed in a sharp new pin-striped gray suit, and was wearing a new felt hat, and new brown-and-white shoes. If I hadn't known Smokey better, I would have though he was dressed to kill.

With him in the front seat was a small dark man wearing colored glasses. In the back seat were two thugs, their breast pockets bulging with steel handkerchiefs.

A large crowd had gathered around the new car.

Smokey sent one of the several children who were dancing around to find Bartlett. Since Bartlett had come back from his kidnaping he spent a lot of time with Karen, but I wasn't invited to join them. I spent my time at Vincent's trying to make up my mind to leave.

Bartlett and Karen came wandering down the street in fifteen minutes. They must have been walking in the outskirts because she was carrying flowers and he was carrying his coat. Walking behind them at a discreet distance was William and walking behind him were the Frasconi brothers. They were still waiting for their boat. When it didn't appear they announced the vendetta was on again.

Smokey called Bartlett over to the car and introduced him to the other occupants. Bartlett called William over.

Bartlett told Karen to have a plate of ice cream with me. Then Smokey and his group and Bartlett and William went upstairs to one of Vincent's rooms.

"Who are they?" Karen asked me.

"Possible business associates," I said.

"They give me goose pimples."

"Karen, you're going to find most people whom Bartlett knows are going to give you goose pimples."

"You don't like him," Karen said.

"I love him like a future brother-in-law. That's not the problem. The fact that you like him is the problem. What exactly are you going to do?"

"Frank said it's only a matter of days before we can leave La Coma. We're going to go to Rome and Florence and maybe settle in Capri."

"Is he going to marry you?"

"Of course. I stopped being a gift a week ago."

I didn't have the heart to tell her that I doubted that Bartlett would ever leave La Coma, nor that I had read a telegram which sealed off his chances of getting any financial help.

In an hour, they came downstairs. Smokey was grinning and shook Bartlett's hand. The man in the smoked glasses grunted.

As the Olds sped off, Bartlett said, "Let's go to the castle." He took Karen with him.

I grabbed William. "What happened upstairs?"

"Be at the docks tomorrow at nine o'clock and you'll find out."

In the evening at dinner, Karen made her second going-away announcement. "I'm going back to the United States to see my mother and arrange a trousseau. Frank says if we're going to live in Capri, I should at least see my mother."

The Principessa said, "How you could choose a Bartelini over a del Grandi is something I'll never understand."

I said good-by to Karen after dinner. I told her if things didn't work out she could always get me at the *News-Press*. She made me promise we would always be friends. I still couldn't figure out how she could have fallen for this bum, but I wished her happiness. The way things were going, she would need a lot of it.

The next morning must have been a sad good-by for everyone. I didn't want any part of it. I saw Karen drive off with William. Then I came downstairs. Bartlett had already left and I started walking down to the port. I noticed other fishermen heading in the same direction. It looked like a mass meeting.

There were about 150 fishermen mingling at the port when I arrived. Pietro was standing on a crate. The men were arguing furiously among themselves. I was about to ask somebody what was up when Pietro shouted for quiet.

"Mr. Bartelini," said Pietro, "wants to speak to you. Before he does, I want to say that I am for his plan, and I think all of you should be for it too."

Bartlett climbed up on the crate. He spotted Pasquale. "You'd better leave, Pasquale," he said. "We don't need you."

Pasquale blushed as the fishermen roared.

"Why can't I stay?"

"Because you're not a fisherman," Pietro shouted.

This brought more howls of laughter from the men and Pasquale went over to his bike and pedaled away.

Now Bartlett turned to the men. "I've called you all here today to offer you a business proposition and a chance to make far more money than you've ever made before. As you all know, I am a rich man. I do not work as hard as any man here and yet I am richer. You have worked, like your fathers and your grandfathers, for the del Grandi family. They pay you nothing and spit in your face. La Coma will always be this way unless you do something about it.

"This is my offer. I want to use you and your boats. I will pay three times what the Principessa pays and you will also receive large bonuses. I won't tell you what I want the boats for. You probably know already. But you'll be working nights out of the heat, and I assure you it will be easier than killing tuna fish."

"What about the Principessa?" a man shouted.

"To hell with the Principessa," Bartlett said. "If we're all in this together, she can't do a thing."

Another voice came from the back. Everyone recognized it as that of the priest. "And what will happen when the contraband police come and confiscate the boats and take the men away to prison? Will you look after their families?"

Many of the men were shaking their heads in agreement.

"The contraband police won't bother us. We are backed by powerful men in Naples. The cargoes will be moved out by morning and no one will be in jeopardy. Everyone will be paid each night and there will be no cheating on the scales. In a month La Coma will be one of the richest towns in Sicily."

The men seemed to approve of that idea.

"It's dishonest work," the priest shouted.

"No more dishonest than working for the Principessa. And I'll tell you what we'll do, Father. We will all contribute to repair the church steeple."

"I don't want it fixed that way," the priest said. "I beg you all not to listen to this man."

Pietro jumped up on the crate next to Bartlett. "If Mr. Bartelini says it's safe, that is good enough for me."

The priest, the Mayor, and a few men left the docks. The others nodded they were in.

"Pietro will be in charge of the boats," Bartlett said. "He is my lieutenant and he will tell you what to do. For the next few days I want you to work on your boats and get them in order.

"Get them painted and the motors in good shape. Not every cruise will be a pleasure trip and we don't want any accidents. Viva La Coma!"

"Viva La Coma!" the men shouted. Bartlett jumped off the crate and was shaking hands. I edged myself over to where he was standing. The hunchback came over and said, "I presume with such an undertaking you will be needing insurance."

"Sure," said Bartlett. "I'm a great believer in insurance."

The hunchback grinned.

When Bartlett left and started up the hill, I fell in beside him. "That's pretty risky business you're getting into, isn't it?" I asked him.

"It's no concern of yours," he said.

"That may be so," I said. "But I have a nice warm spot in my heart for Karen and if you're going to marry her I'd hate to see her spending the rest of her life bringing you food in the clink."

Bartlett walked along for a few minutes and then said, "I'm not going to marry Karen. She doesn't know it, but she's not coming back."

"What?"

"Pete," said Bartlett, "I've done some pretty lousy things in my time. But I've never been in love before. When I finally fell in love it was too late.

"Maybe I would never have fallen in love if I had stayed

in the States. I was too big a man for love then. This is no life for any dame and I'm a little late in trying to settle down. So I've sent her home. She thinks it's just to see her mother, but when she gets there she'll find a letter telling her the whole thing is off."

"I owe you an apology," I said. "I thought you were a one hundred per cent heel. But there's still hope even for you."

"Anyway," said Bartlett, "this cigarette business is just a start. The man with the smoked glasses assured me he could get me to Naples. Life isn't over for me yet. I got to make a success of this so I can move on. When are you leaving?"

"That's a funny thing," I said. "Just when I think I've got the finish to my story, something else happens and I can't leave."

"Don't you file anything on this business!" Bartlett said.

"I'm a man of discretion," I assured him.

When we got back to the castle, we discovered the Principessa and Alfredo had gone to Palermo for a week. It was a break for Bartlett. William returned from Palermo that evening and said he had put Karen on the boat.

"She told me," William said to Bartlett, "that you were going in the ice-cream business with Smokey and the guys from Naples. Did you tell her that?"

"Yeah," said Bartlett. "I told her that."

William laughed. "She asked me what I was going to do in the ice-cream factory and I said I was going to dip the popsicles into the chocolate."

"What's so damn funny about that?" Bartlett said.

156

"Nothing, boss. I'm sorry."

Bartlett got soused that night and William and I had to carry him to his room.

The next week was spent in preparations for the cigarette-smuggling operation. The Naples gang had sent a speedy motorboat for Bartlett to use. He made Pietro his crew member. Bartlett held boat drills every day with a stop watch as well as simulated loadings and unloadings. He had each boat owner cut a panel in his boat just above the water line and he ordered them to round up chains which he had them clean and oil. Then he pretended he was the contraband police and the fishermen had to dump their cargoes of cigarettes through the hatch on the chains they had gathered.

"Remember this," he told them. "If they don't find cigarettes on board, they can't do anything to you."

Those that didn't own boats were hired as stevedores to unload the cargoes onto the trucks. In less than a week, Bartlett had the entire operation running smoothly. I had to admire him for his ability to organize the men.

When Bartlett was ready he sent word to Smokey, and Smokey and the Neapolitan big shot arrived. Bartlett held a night demonstration for them and they must have been impressed.

William told me the first operation would take place the next evening.

I wasn't allowed on any of the boats, not that I wanted to be, so I just hung around with the stevedores and some of the wives who were nervously standing by the docks. The women didn't like what their men were doing and the priest expressed his displeasure in no uncertain terms at Sunday Mass.

The boats left La Coma at midnight. They returned at five in the morning loaded with cases of cigarettes. Trucks suddenly started arriving at four and there was a great deal of activity. I tried to stay out of the way.

Bartlett's practice runs had paid off and by seven o'clock there wasn't a case of cigarettes or a truck on the dock.

It had obviously been a strain on the men and some of them looked very pale as they stood in line waiting for Pietro to pay them. Bartlett was the last to arrive with William.

"It went okay?" I said.

"We have to start out earlier," he said.

He looked over at the men and their women. They still looked pretty frightened.

"Let's have a fiesta tonight," Bartlett yelled at Pietro. The next shipment wasn't expected for three days.

The people cheered and the tension was relaxed.

We were all pretty tired by the time we got back to the castle and were looking forward to a bath and some sleep.

But just before we crossed the drawbridge, the Principessa came out on the balcony, the very same balcony her ancestor had used, and screamed, "Communists! You're all Communists!"

We looked up at the outraged woman.

"So you think you can take my fishermen away and destroy my tuna? Well, nobody can do that to the del Grandis. You swine," and she uttered Italian curse words I had never heard before.

Then she went to Bartlett's room and started throwing his things out of the window. Most of them fell in the moat. She then ran to my room and did the same thing. I watched in horror as my new Olivetti went soaring out the window into the moat.

"I want to talk to you," Bartlett yelled at her.

"Talk to me, do you?" she said.

She disappeared and when she came back on the balcony she had a shotgun in her hands and aimed it at us.

"Talk to her later," William said, taking off at full steam. I was not far behind him and Bartlett was just at my heels. She fired both barrels and screamed, "You won't get away with it, Bartelini. You won't get away with it."

We didn't stop running until we got near the town.

William said, "She was kind of mad."

Bartlett said, "Serves her right, the old bitch. She's finally getting what was coming to her."

"I'd be worried about her," I said. "The vengeance of the del Grandis, you know."

"She can't hurt us," Bartlett said.

"How are we going to get our stuff?" William asked.

"We'll send the hunchback up for it. It should be included in the price of insurance."

"My poor typewriter," I said.

"Maybe I can get one of the captains to bring you one from Tangiers," Bartlett said.

"Our main problem now," William said, "is where to sleep."

"Let's sleep on the boat," Bartlett said. "There's a cabin there and I'd like to be close to the operation anyway. Sorry, Pete. We don't have any room for you."

"I'll stay at Vincent's. I haven't suffered in a long, long time."

"When we get some time," William said brightly, "why don't we burn the castle? It would teach her a lesson."

"The damn thing is so full of mildew," Bartlett said, "it probably wouldn't burn."

# 16

THAT evening La Coma held a fiesta. The square had been lighted as before but the food was far more lavish than anything served the night we arrived. There was plenty of wine to drink and it was apparent the men had spent much of their earnings from the morning to celebrate.

Bartlett was at the seat of honor at the head table. When I found him he was drunk.

"She was the most wonderful girl in the world," he said, slobbering all over me.

"Yeah. She sure was."

"I shouldn't have let her go."

"You made a mistake."

"You loved her too, didn't you, Pete?"

"Sure, Frank. I was nuts about her. But the best man won."

"The best man lost," Bartlett said. "I don't have her."

"In the long run, it's probably better. You'll find another girl in Italy."

Bartlett threw a bottle against the wall. "I'll never find another girl like Karen. *Never*."

"Okay. Okay."

Someone handed Bartlett another bottle of wine and he drank some more.

Then he said, "Let's have some dancing." He grabbed a woman and started to dance. She protested, "It's forbidden . . . it's forbidden."

"Nothing's forbidden any more," Bartlett said. "I'm running this show."

The rest of the people in the square were shocked, but in a few minutes they were all dancing and the square was filled with laughing, shouting men and women.

I saw the Principessa standing on the outskirts of the crowd and I walked over to her and said hello.

"I didn't have anything to do with the boats, Principessa," I said. "I wish you hadn't thrown my typewriter into the moat."

"My troubles started the day you all arrived," she muttered. "They think they have me defeated, but they haven't."

The Principessa suddenly pushed her way through the crowd. She was standing in the middle of the square shouting at everyone to stop dancing.

When they saw who it was they all became frightened and pretty soon the entire square was hushed into silence.

"You are wicked, wicked people," the Principessa shrilled. "You have been taken in by an American gangster and he will send you all to the devil before you are finished. I will forgive your sinfulness if you wish to return and

162

work for me. The tuna are running again, and there is work for all of you."

Bartlett staggered over to where the Principessa was standing. "No witches are allowed at a fiesta," he said. "The fishermen made more money this morning than they make from you in a month. You will have to kill the tuna yourself. You can do it, too, with that mouth of yours."

The people in the square laughed.

The Principessa slapped Bartlett in the face. "All right. I gave everyone a chance. Now you will be sorry. The del Grandis can meet any situation. But when you do come back to me, you will be crawling like turtles. Most of you owe me money for your boats. I want the money right away."

"And you'll get it right away, you old bitch," Bartlett cried. "I will give any man here who owes this praying mantis the lire to pay off the debt. To hell with the del Grandis," he said, lifting his wine bottle.

The people chimed in, "To hell with the del Grandis."

The Principessa spat and walked out of the square, pushing aside anyone who got in her way.

Pietro, who was feeling no pain, came out on the square and shouted, "Let's drink to Frank Bartelini! He promised us prosperity and he gave it to us."

The party lasted all night. In the morning, everyone was fast asleep, except the children and the tuna and the Principessa.

There were three deliveries of cigarettes that week.

By the time the third one came in, I had pieced together the operation.

Naples let Bartlett know when a cargo boat from Tangiers would stop by outside the La Coma harbor. The boat anchored ten or fifteen miles offshore. Bartlett went out first in his speedboat and boarded the vessel. He paid over in American dollars for the cigarettes. In the meantime, the fishing boats were arriving. They circled the ship until Bartlett flashed a green light and then each one in turn came up to be loaded and sent away. I also found out the shore operations were run by the Mafia, who supplied the trucks and the hiding places. Distribution throughout the island was made by different operators who bought directly from the Mafia.

Naples apparently was paid directly by the Mafia and they, in turn, sent money over to Bartlett. From William I discovered Bartlett's share was only 15 per cent. The deal had been made after his kidnaping and the Naples people knew they could make any kind of proposition they wanted to.

The fact that the Mafia was so actively engaged in the enterprise gave Bartlett a sense of security. Naples had also assured him that nothing would happen and after the first three trips they seemed to be right.

But from facts I learned later on, the Principessa wasn't taking this lying down. She disappeared mysteriously after the fiesta and no one saw her for a week. Someone said she had gone to Rome. Others more hopefully said she had thrown herself into the volcano of Mt. Etna.

The paper was badgering me to come home. They felt I had spent enough time and money in Italy and they wanted the series.

But I could smell something was going to happen and I ignored their messages.

It happened on the fourth trip. I no longer kept an all-night vigil, preferring to sleep instead. I had decided to wait another week and, if nothing happened, I would return to New York. It was about seven o'clock in the morning when I heard shouting and screaming outside my hotel window in Vincent's. I opened the window and looked out. Women and children were all running toward the port. I got dressed, grabbed my camera and rushed down the hill. When I got to the dock, I saw a large crowd of women screaming and crying and looking out to sea. Far off, I could see the La Coma fishing fleet but they seemed to be heading toward Palermo.

I saw the Mayor there, trying to comfort some of the women.

"What happened?" I asked.

"The contraband police. We think they caught our men."

We saw one boat headed toward the La Coma dock. I recognized it as Bartlett's speedboat. Pietro was at the wheel and William and Bartlett were standing on the deck. Pietro brought the boat into dock and the women and children rushed forward.

Everyone tried to speak at once. Tears were rolling down Pietro's face.

Bartlett shouted, "It's all a mistake. I'll have your men out by tonight."

This confirmed the rumor and the women wailed and screamed.

Then they turned their sorrow into anger and screamed and cursed Bartlett. William was standing with a machine gun next to Bartlett, but that didn't stop the women. Several tried to attack him. I was busy with my camera. If Bartlett was going to be lynched, I at least wanted a shot of it.

But the priest arrived on the scene and calmed the women down. "I will go to Palermo," he shouted over their wailing, "and find out how long it will be."

Pietro was crying in earnest now. The priest turned to Bartlett. "You have brought a curse on La Coma. May God forgive me for what I think of you."

The priest kept pushing the women and children up the hill toward town.

I wandered over to the boat. Bartlett had disappeared into the cabin, William was on deck. He seemed pretty unnerved by the women.

I asked what had happened.

"We went out about eleven, but bad luck dogged us from the start. First we couldn't find the boat. Then when we did, the boss and the English captain had an argument over the cargo. The boss had broken open a case of cigarettes and found some of them had been in salt water. We had to check all the cases, which took some time.

"On our way back we suddenly heard sirens. None of the boats did anything we had trained them to do. A loudspeaker sounded and warned them they were surrounded and would be shot at.

"The boss shouted to the other boats to disperse and dump their cigarettes, but they didn't. Then the boss

166

grabbed the wheel from Pietro and we were off like a shot. They fired at us but we were too fast for them. Besides, they couldn't have done anything to us if they'd caught us. We didn't have a cigarette on board. We hid out in a cove and then when we saw the boats were heading toward Palermo, we came here. We should have stayed in the cove."

"I wonder," I said, "how the contraband police found out."

"As far as I'm concerned," William said, "I'm all for pulling out today and trying to make it to Tangiers."

"What about Bartlett?"

"He's in a state of shock."

# 17

I WANDERED around La Coma in the afternoon. It was like a ghost town. The only noise I heard was the wailing and praying that came from the open door of the church. The children seemed to have disappeared and the hot, dusty square was barren of life. A town without men can be a frightening thing.

I went over to the town hall. The Mayor was in his office and I stopped by to see him. He looked tired and haggard and discouraged.

"We don't even have the money to pay for a lawyer," the Mayor said.

"Did the priest inform on the people?"

"No," said the Mayor. "The priest is a strict man, but he loves the people. He wouldn't do that."

"Then who was it?"

"Look up the hill, to the castle of the del Grandis, and you won't have to look any further. The Principessa would never let Bartelini take her fishermen away. The del Grandis have relatives in Rome. I am sure it was she who brought the contraband police to La Coma."

"What's going to happen now?" I asked the Mayor.

"The priest and I will go to Palermo tomorrow morning. We will beg for the men's release. Perhaps they will let them go. But the boats—they will take the boats—and what good will the men be without their boats?"

"Can I ride in to Palermo with you tomorrow?"

"We are taking the bus. Anyone may ride the bus."

I went outside and found William carrying a crate of food.

"What are you doing?"

William looked around to see if anyone could hear us talking and then said in a low voice, "We're clearing out tomorrow morning. We're going to try to make it to Tangiers. This town is ready to explode. If the fishermen are freed, we may get lynched."

"Where's Bartlett?"

"He's down in the boat. He wants to turn himself in. He thinks if he turns himself in they'll free the other men, but I told him he was nuts. I have to get him out of here before he goes off his rocker."

"Why don't you clear out, William, and leave Bartlett to his fate?" I asked him.

"Leave the boss here? What kind of a bum do you think I am? The boss didn't do nothing wrong. He gave the people work, they had money, they were happy. They got no kicks coming."

William was about to leave when Inspector Ruffino drove up with a carload of uniformed policemen. He stopped in front of us.

"Where is Bartelini?" he said.

William didn't reply.

Ruffino said to me, "Where is he?"

"Down at the docks."

"Both of you get into the car," he ordered.

We squeezed in and Ruffino pointed the way to the docks.

The car pulled up in front of the motorboat and the police jumped out.

Bartlett was sitting on the deck. He didn't bother to look up as we came over.

"I want to speak to you, Bartelini," Ruffino yelled.

Bartlett didn't answer.

Ruffino jumped on the deck of the boat and pulled Bartlett roughly to his feet. "Get off this boat!"

Bartlett didn't move and Ruffino pushed him. I thought Bartlett was going to fall into the water, but two of the policemen caught him and pulled him on the dock. Ruffino jumped off the boat and yelled, "When I tell you to do something, you do it!"

Bartlett spat on the ground and Ruffino suddenly swung at him and knocked him down.

William tried to jump in and help, but two of the policemen held him.

"Get up!"

Bartlett got up and Ruffino swung again. The blow connected and Bartlett went down again. His eye was closed and there was a cut over the cheek.

Ruffino stood over Bartlett. "Thanks to you, one hundred and fifty men are in prison and they will lose their boats and their families will starve. I should have sent you to Ustica when you first arrived.

"Get up! I'm not going to hit you any more."

Bartlett got to his feet.

"What are you doing with this boat?" Ruffino asked.

"It's mine."

"You're not allowed to own a boat," said Ruffino, turning to a policeman. "See that no one goes on board."

William was struggling with the men who were holding him.

"What nationality are you?" Ruffino asked William.

"I'm an American."

"Then go back to America. I'm going to give you an escort to see that you leave on the next available plane. If America can send us Italian-born gangsters, then we can send them American-born ones."

Ruffino looked over at me.

I raised my hand. "I had nothing to do with this, Inspector. The Mayor will testify to that."

Ruffino hesitated and then turned to Bartlett.

"I'm going to be staying here for a little while, Bartelini, for the sole purpose of watching you. If you make one mistake—just one—I'll throw you into prison for life."

"Where am I going to sleep if you won't let me sleep on the boat?"

"After what you've done to these people," Ruffino said, "I don't see how you can sleep."

"Can I get my belongings?" Bartlett asked.

Ruffino nodded and Bartlett went into the cabin.

While Bartlett was gathering his things I managed to

talk Ruffino into giving me a note to the chief of police in Palermo so I could visit the prison.

In twenty minutes, Bartlett climbed out of the boat with his suitcase. William tried to help him carry it, but Ruffino said, "Let him carry it."

Ruffino ordered William to stay by the boat until the next morning under guard of one of his men.

"So long, boss," William said, and I thought this big hunk of a man was going to break down. "I'll be in touch."

Bartlett shook his hand, took his suitcase and started into the town. I walked with him. As we trudged up the cobblestoned hill, women opened their windows and shouted curses at Bartlett. Children appeared in doorways, screaming, "Papa, papa."

Someone threw a pail of dirty water out of the window and it just missed us. Bartlett looked straight ahead. I offered to help him with his bag, but he shrugged me off.

When we arrived in the square we walked slowly over to Vincent's. Pasquale and the Mayor were sitting at a table and Vincent was serving them. No one looked at Bartlett.

"Can I have a room?" Bartlett asked.

"All the rooms are filled," Vincent snarled.

"I'll pay you double," Bartlett said.

"Why don't you give the money to the women whose husbands are in prison?" the Mayor said.

"Watch my bag, will you Pasquale?" Bartlett said.

Pasquale shook his head. "I'm busy."

"I'll watch it, Frank," I said.

Bartlett dropped the bag and walked up the hill to the castle. Fifteen minutes later we heard a shotgun report and ten minutes after that Bartlett reappeared.

"It sounded like she had no rooms to rent," I said.

Bartlett sat on his bag and wiped his face. I was tempted to take a photo of him, but I was too embarrassed.

"Maybe your aunt would put you up," I said.

"Yeah. Maybe," Bartlett muttered. "Where does my aunt live?" he asked the Mayor.

The Mayor ignored him.

"Where does his aunt live?" I asked the Mayor.

"The second street on the left," he said to me. "It's the fourth house on the left."

Bartlett got up and I picked up his bag for him.

We found the house. It wasn't really a house, but a large one-room clay hut. There were beds along the sides, and the walls were covered with religious medallions and pictures of saints. In the corner was a small stove where the cooking was done, and in the center of the hut was a table. Bartlett's aunt and cousins were sitting around the table eating platefuls of rice.

"Can he stay here?" I asked when Bartlett didn't say anything.

His aunt looked at the other children and then replied, "You can sleep in Eduardo's bed. He is in prison." She started to cry.

I carried the bag over to the bed she indicated.

"Do you want anything to eat?" one of the children asked sullenly.

Bartlett shook his head, and lay down on the bed.

I didn't want to hang around, so I said, "Thanks," and ducked out.

I spent the afternoon writing the story of a town that had been arrested. It was news, and probably the wire services had already filed the details. I was sure Simpson was blowing a gasket waiting for my version.

After I filed it, I bought a bottle of wine and went to see Bartlett.

He was still lying on the bed. The family was in church except for Gisella. She was ironing some clothes. I gave Bartlett the wine and he took a long drink.

"How many people live in this hut?" I asked Gisella.

"When my father was alive, seven."

Bartlett was sitting up. For the first time he seemed to notice the surroundings.

"Did my parents live in a place like this?" Bartlett asked.

"They lived in the house next door," the cousin said bitterly.

"No wonder they left La Coma," Bartlett said.

Gisella looked at him, her eyes flashing. "Yes, they left. Mamma and Papa were happy when they left. They knew America had hope for them. Your papa promised if he ever found the money, he would send for my parents. Your papa wrote all the time, but he never had the money. But my parents always loved him because they knew if he had the money, he would have sent for them.

"Then your papa died, and my parents decided there was no hope of them ever going to America. But one day we read in an Italian magazine that you had become a rich man, and we were happy for you. After my papa died, my mother asked me to write to you and ask you to lend us the money to come to the United States. Mamma was sure that you, being the son of your father, would help us. But you never answered the letters.

"Then war came to Sicily," Gisella continued. "Mamma thought it was because of the war that we did not hear from you. Afterward the American soldiers occupied La Coma. There was one soldier, a nice Italian boy from California. He saw how we lived here and he promised when he went back he would stop off in New York and explain how bad things were for us.

"He tried to keep his promise. He wrote he went to your apartment but they always said you were out. Then he found where you went to dinner and he waited outside the restaurant. He tried to talk to you, but your friends beat him up. He said you were no good."

"I'm sorry," said Bartlett. "I didn't know."

"And now," cried Gisella, "our brother is in prison because of you."

I was pretty embarrassed and didn't know what to say.

I turned to Bartlett. "I'm going to Palermo tomorrow. Do you want anything?"

"Yeah. Bring back a gun so I can blow my brains out."

There was an interesting group of people going to Palermo on the bus the next morning. There were the priest and the Mayor, William with a police escort, myself and Pietro, who decided he was going to turn himself in.

I sat next to William. He was pretty downcast.

"I would rather have left him in Alcatraz," William said.

"It would have been more merciful," I agreed. "What are your plans, William?"

"I don't know. I doubt if the boys will want me hanging

175

around. But I'm a good valet. I could work for some legitimate family."

"Don't do that, William. You could never stand it."

"Are you going to write about the boss?" William asked.

"That was the whole idea."

"Don't be too rough on him," he pleaded.

"I have to write it the way it happened."

"You write the whole thing the way it happened and nobody will believe you."

"On that point, William, I'm afraid you're right."

When we got off at Palermo, I said good-by to William as he was whisked off to the airport. The priest and Mayor went to see a lawyer and I went to see the chief of police. Pietro went with me, but when he entered the police barracks and demanded to be arrested, the police refused. He said he was guilty of smuggling cigarettes, but the police threw him out.

Pietro was crying in front of the station. "Tell them, Signore," he begged of me, "that I am the most guilty."

I didn't feel that was my function so I didn't say anything.

I left him sobbing on the sidewalk and went into the chief's office.

He told me that he wasn't sure what would happen with the men but the case would be held a few days later. At first he didn't want me to see the prisoners, but after I showed him Ruffino's note he agreed I could talk to one of them.

"What will happen to the men?" I asked him.

"We're going to have to fine them," the chief said. "If

they can pay the fine, we'll let them out of prison and they can have their boats back."

"Will it be a stiff fine?"

"That isn't for me to decide. But we must make an example of La Coma or every other fishing village in Sicily will go into the cigarette-smuggling business."

"And if they can't pay the fine?"

The chief of police indicated there was nothing he could do.

I went to the prison with my pass and asked to see Eduardo. He said the men were all right, and not bitter about their fate. A few of them wanted to implicate Bartlett, but the others wouldn't let them. The rule of Sicily is *omerta*, or, "never tell the police anything."

I assured Eduardo they wouldn't have to stay in prison long. I was giving out false hopes, but I couldn't think of anything else to say.

Eduardo thanked me and was taken out. As I walked out of the prison yard, I saw the police bring in Pietro. He was handcuffed but happy.

"They wouldn't arrest me for smuggling cigarettes," Pietro yelled, "so I made them arrest me for hitting one of them.

"Viva La Coma!" Pietro shouted in the yard.

From inside the prison I heard the voices of a hundred men shouting, "Viva La Coma!" The police pushed Pietro roughly along, but the shouting inside the prison continued.

I went over to the AP stringer's office and read what

he had filed on the story. His version intimated Bartlett was behind the operation.

"What kind of a play did the story get?" I asked the AP man.

"We hit the whole country," he said. "Any story that mentions Bartlett gets a play."

I decided to put in a collect call to Simpson.

It took twenty-four hours to get through.

"When are you coming back?" he wanted to know.

"I'd like to hang around and see what's going to happen to La Coma," I said. "Did you get my story?"

"Yeah, but we want the series. It's hot as hell now and Lucas and Boyle are anxious that you get back and write it."

"I'll be back in a week," I promised.

"At the latest," Simpson said.

"You'd better send me some more dough," I said.

"I can't hear you," Simpson replied.

"*I need more money*," I hollered.

"It must be this phone connection."

"Don't be a wise guy, Harry. I'm broke."

"Lucas won't let me send you anything. Come on home!"

I said some things into the phone system that the Italians were going to have difficulty translating.

# 18

DESPITE the pleas of a lawyer who had volunteered to help, and the pledges of the priest and the Mayor that it would never happen again, a fine of 30,000,000 lire ($50,000) was imposed on the men of La Coma. The men and the boats would be released if the fine was paid. If not, the men would have to stay in prison, and each one would be individually tried, a process that might take years.

The Mayor and the priest left for La Coma to break the sad news to the families. I got disgusted suddenly with the whole mess and, since the *News-Press* didn't give a damn, I decided to return to the United States. The next day, I went out to the airport to take a plane to Rome, where I had a flight to New York arranged.

I was in the restaurant of the airport idly watching a plane that had just landed discharge a bunch of passengers when I saw a familiar mink coat.

"Karen," I yelled, running out on the field. I threw my arms around her. "What are you doing here?"

"I read about what happened in La Coma," she said. "It's awful. I had to come back."

"Didn't you get Frank's letter?"

"Yes, I got it," she said. "But I couldn't stay away. How is he?"

"Pretty bad," I said. "He's on the verge of blowing his brains out."

"I've got to see him."

"It won't do any good unless you know where you can get your hands on fifty thousand dollars."

"Has he been kidnaped again?" Karen asked.

"No," I told her. "That's the fine they're demanding for the hundred and fifty fishermen."

"What are you doing here?" Karen asked as an after-thought.

"I'm going back to America. And you had better, too. Believe me, there's nothing you can do for Frank."

"I've got to see him. If he tells me he doesn't want me to stay, I'll go home with you."

"Is that a promise?" I said.

"It's a promise."

Like an idiot, I rode back to La Coma on the bus with her.

We found Frank in his aunt's hut. There were now empty bottles of wine around the bed, and he hadn't shaved since I left him there. The rest of the family, when they saw Karen, left the hut.

Karen ran over to Bartlett and tried to kiss him.

He recognized her through his alcoholic haze, and pushed her away.

"Who told you to come back?" he said.

"Darling, the fishermen, the people. What are you going to do?"

"There's nothing to do," Bartlett said drunkenly. "I hope when they get out they kill me. I don't have the guts to do it myself."

"You've got to help them," Karen cried.

"I can't help them," Bartlett said. "I can't help anybody. Get out of here. I told you not to come back. I don't want anything to do with you, don't you understand? Go marry Shakespeare over there and let me get drunk in peace."

I helped Karen up and she walked out of the hut, dazed.

"I told you," I said.

"What are we going to do?" Karen asked.

"There isn't anything to do except go back to America," I said. "You promised."

We walked into the square. Inspector Ruffino was sitting at Vincent's. He stood up and bowed when he saw Karen. We both nodded and sat at another table.

I ordered two ice creams.

"Pete, we've got to think of something," Karen said.

"What can we do?"

"Maybe the United States would lend La Coma the money."

"I'm afraid even the U.S. won't give loans to bail people out of jail."

As we talked, the hunchback walked by and waved.

"I wonder if he's had any good kidnapings lately?" I said.

Karen sat up straight. "Kidnaping! That's the answer."

She looked over to where Ruffino was sitting and whispered, "Let's take a walk."

She dragged me away from the café.

"How much is an American citizen worth?" she asked.

"Huh?"

"Just give me a guess."

"I don't have the slightest idea."

"Do you think the U.S. Government would be willing to pay $50,000 for one of its citizens?"

"How the hell do I know?"

"Well, I know," Karen said, "and especially if the victim is a woman.

"Suppose," she continued excitedly, "I was kidnaped by Mondello. And suppose he asked for $50,000 ransom, and instead of keeping the money, he gave it to me to pay the fine. What's wrong with that?"

I stopped Karen in her tracks. "Who is going to pay this ransom?"

"The American government, of course. After you write the horror stories they'll be forced to pay. The American people couldn't stand to have one of their virgin daughters kidnaped by a Sicilian bandit."

"But, Karen," I protested. "If anyone finds out what we've done . . . it's embezzlement! We can go to jail!"

"We're not keeping the money," Karen said. "We're giving it back to the Italian Government. What's the difference if we give them the money or the American Government gives it to them?"

"Mondello would never do it," I said. "What's in it for

him, except they may kill him?"

Karen thought this over for a moment. "I know," she said. "We'll ask for $75,000 ransom. We'll give Mondello $25,000 for his trouble."

"It'll never work," I said. "Let's go back to America."

"What kind of newspaperman are you?" Karen cried. "This is a big story for you either way."

She didn't wait for a reply and dashed toward the pier with me following at her heels.

We found the hunchback and Karen said to me, "Tell him I want to be kidnaped."

The hunchback looked at both of us as if we were crazy. "What for?"

Karen nudged me. "For ransom."

Then I explained Karen's plan to the hunchback.

The hunchback listened in fascination. But when I was finished he shook his head. "Mondello would never agree. He has never kidnaped a woman or a foreigner. It's against everything he stands for."

"But," I said, "it's different. In this case the victim wants to be kidnaped. She's begging for it. This is for the people of La Coma. You love La Coma, don't you?"

The hunchback said he did.

"Then you must help the people get back their boats and their men out of prison. You owe it to them."

The hunchback was doubtful but he told us he would see what he could do.

He reported back the next day. "Mondello doesn't like the idea at all. He said he has no facilities for kidnaping a woman."

"I'll rough it," Karen said.

The hunchback shook his head. "The risk is too great. The authorities would never stand for a foreigner being kidnaped. The hills would be flooded with troops, and they would be merciless if they caught him."

I told Karen what he said, and Karen said, "Write a note for me to Mondello."

I took out a pencil and my pad.

"Dear Mr. Mondello," she dictated. "I have never asked anyone to kidnap me before and I would not be kidnaped except by someone as kind and understanding as you.

"I know you are a son of La Coma and therefore you must be as disturbed as we all are over the horrible thing the police have done. I ask you to take me, so we can free the men of La Coma from prison. You will be paid for the kidnaping, but I know money is not the main object in your life. You have a soul and your soul rests with the people of La Coma.

"The authorities are holding our men . . ."

"Our men?" I interrupted.

"Just write what I tell you," Karen begged. ". . . our men, and there is no way to raise the fine unless the United States pays it. But they won't unless I am kidnaped.

"I promise I won't be any trouble, and furthermore, if you are caught, I will say I ran away with you because I love you. Please, please, for the sake of La Coma, for the sake of one who admires you, let me be kidnaped by you. It will only be for a short time."

I wrote it all down and Karen signed it. She gave it to the hunchback to deliver to Mondello.

Two days later we met again and the hunchback said, "Mondello agrees to it. But he doesn't like it. He says he's only doing it for La Coma."

Karen threw her arms around the hunchback. "Oh, thank you, thank you."

It was decided that Karen would be kidnaped the following evening.

I insisted on going with her to Mondello's headquarters and the hunchback told us to meet him by the shrine. We decided not to let Bartlett in on the plan, as he would only try to stop Karen.

Why was I doing all this? I loved Karen and would have jumped in the Bay of Sicily if she had asked me to. Besides, the idea was so crazy it might work.

When we arrived at the statue of the Madonna, two men appeared from the bushes. They grabbed both of us, though they did it gently, and placed us on horses. This time we were not blindfolded.

"Follow me," one of the men said.

A welcome committee was waiting for us at Mondello's headquarters. It had been completely cleaned up since the last time we were there.

The shack had been painted, the holes repaired so you couldn't see in, and flowers had been planted around it.

Mondello, beaming, escorted us over to the shack. Inside was a brass bed with two white sheets and two woolen blankets. An American flag had been hung over the bed, and around on the walls Mondello had tacked old *Saturday Evening Post* covers. A wash basin and a dressing table were also in the shack.

Next to the shack, Mondello had installed a homemade shower with an empty gasoline drum and a curtain.

"It's beautiful," Karen said. "How can I ever thank you?"

Mondello looked very pleased.

I said to Mondello, "Let's get the ransom note written. I better get back to town before someone misses me."

I showed him the draft of a note I had prepared. It read: "Unless I am paid $75,000 I will kill the American citizen Karen Withers."

Mondello read the note and became angry. "I could never write such a letter. How could Giuseppe Mondello say that he would kill a woman?"

"Well, what do you want to say?"

"Say that unless I get $75,000 Karen Withers will never be seen again."

"That's good enough," I said. "Now you must write it and sign it. Have your men post it on the door of the town hall. I'll go back to La Coma and write my story. I'll be back in a week or so. I trust you, Mondello."

"She will be safer with me than in an American Embassy," Mondello assured me.

We shook hands.

I went over to Karen. "Are you all right?"

"Of course I'm all right," she said. "And this will be a wonderful chance to practice my Italian."

I kissed her.

Mondello came over. "Please, don't be too long. I'm not sure I like this business."

I rode back to La Coma with the guide and I wrote my story before I went to sleep.

186

Nothing happened that night, but the next morning, when I woke up, I saw dozens of people in the square.

"What happened?" I shouted from the window.

A little boy yelled up, "The American girl has been kidnaped by Mondello."

Vincent yelled up, "He's asking $75,000 in ransom. The man is crazy!"

I got dressed and rushed downstairs.

The Mayor was talking to a group of women. "I can't understand it. Mondello has never kidnaped a woman before."

"Or a foreigner," someone added.

Pasquale was standing around, looking embarrassed. A voice cried, "You must go find her, Pasquale. It is your duty."

"I will stay here," Pasquale said, "and protect the women and children."

Inspector Ruffino was standing in front of the post office when I went over to send my first kidnaping story, which I had written the previous day.

He was smoking a cigarette. "The vigilant press is on the job, I see," he said.

"I'm just going to file the story on the kidnaping," I said.

Ruffino looked at the seven carefully typed pages.

"You are a very fast writer," he observed, "to have a seven-page story so soon after the kidnaping was announced. May I look at it?"

"No," I said. "We have a rule that no one can see a story until it's in print."

"You've met Mondello," Ruffino said. "Don't you think it's strange he kidnaped an American . . . a woman . . .

something he has never done before?"

"Maybe," I said, "he fell in love with her. Or maybe she went with him willingly. You know how American girls are bound to romanticize bandits."

"Seventy-five thousand dollars is an awful lot of money. Where could the girl possibly get it?"

"I don't know," I said. "All I deal in is the facts."

"I wonder if that's all you deal in," he said.

I went into the post office without replying.

When I came out of the post office I found Bartlett, still looking as disheveled as he had in the hut, but apparently sobered up, yelling at Ruffino.

"You've got to find her," he was shouting. "He'll kill her, he'll rape her! There's no telling what the maniac will do."

"I'm sure she is being treated well," Ruffino said.

"What makes you so sure?"

"Just a hunch. Inspectors are great for hunches."

"Let's go after him," Bartlett pleaded. "Give me a gun. I'll kill the son-of-a-bitch."

"I can't give you a gun," Ruffino said. "Please believe me, Signor Bartelini, no harm will come to her. If we send troops into the mountains, Mondello could possibly panic. Let's wait a few days and see what happens."

"Inspector," pleaded Bartlett, "I'm not asking anything for myself. You can send me to Ustica or to the pen in Palermo, but you've got to help her. I'm responsible for her being here. I love her. Give me a gun. I'll go after her myself."

"I'm sorry, Signor Bartelini."

Ruffino walked away.

Bartlett saw me standing in the doorway.

"Pete," he said, grabbing my jacket. "Mondello has Karen."

"I know," I replied. "I just sent the story."

"We've got to save her," Bartlett said.

"Don't try it, Frank." I said. "You might get Karen killed."

# 19

THE rest of this story I had to piece together from many sources, all of them, I might add, reliable. Everything took place so fast it wasn't until after it was all over that I was able to realize what had happened.

My story appeared in New York, but instead of causing the sensation we thought it would, every other paper in town tried to knock it down.

After the *News-Press* printed my story on the front page, the other papers went to town. One of them printed Karen's photo on page three, with a caption: KIDNAPING OR PUBLICITY STUNT? The story said that friends of Karen Withers had said she wanted to be in the movies, and there was a strong suspicion that Karen's kidnaping was a publicity stunt.

The other papers and television commentators took the same line. Winchell called Karen the "Marie McDonald of the year" and the State Department said they would not get involved unless the kidnaping was confirmed by the Italian Foreign Office.

Simpson called me in La Coma and he was burning on the phone. "We've got a hot potato on our hands. Is that kidnaping story a phony?"

"Hell, no," I said. "It's true. The girl was snatched and he's asking $75,000 ransom. I swear it."

"Everyone denies it," said Simpson. "The State Department, the Italian Foreign Office and the police. You get some confirmation, boy, and get it fast."

The connection was broken.

I stared into the receiver for a moment and then left the post office. I walked over to see Ruffino, who had taken the Mayor's office in the town hall for his headquarters.

Ruffino offered me a cigarette.

"Nobody believes me," I said. "Inspector, haven't you notified Rome?"

"No," said Ruffino. "I was waiting for further developments."

"You have to confirm it," I said. "They're saying it's a publicity stunt in the United States and it's not."

Ruffino said, "What is it?"

"It's not a publicity stunt. Don't ask me to explain it, but we have a chance of getting the men of La Coma freed and their boats back. It's the only chance. Bartlett has nothing to do with this."

"If I send word to Rome they'll send troops in and hunt for Mondello in earnest. Do you want that?"

"Sicily is a big place," I pleaded. "If you were in charge of the search you could send the men in any direction."

Ruffino excused himself for a few minutes and then returned.

"All right," he said. "I'll confirm your kidnaping. I'll send a cable to Rome. But I'm warning you why I'm doing it. I am going to take Mondello alive and you and Miss Withers are going to lead me to him. Mondello is playing a stupid game and he's going to swing for it. My troops will find Mondello."

He slammed his fist hard on the desk.

I got out in a hurry, but I was disturbed by Ruffino's threats. I would have to be very careful.

Ruffino did notify Rome, and the Foreign Ministry notified the American Ambassador, who notified the State Department.

I received a cable from Lucas himself: CONGRATULATIONS. WE BEAT EVERY PAPER IN COUNTRY BY FORTY-EIGHT HOURS. STAY WITH STORY GIVING EVERY DETAIL. BOYLE SAYS HE'S SOLD TWO HUNDRED FIFTY NEWSPAPERS ON YOUR SERIES AND ORDERS STILL COMING IN. AM INCREASING YOUR SALARY BY TWENTY-FIVE REPEAT TWENTY-FIVE DOLLARS A WEEK. KEEP THE COPY COMING.

Good old Lucas, I thought to myself. No one could say he wasn't a fast guy with a buck. It was my first raise in three years.

I cabled back: THANKS. SUGGEST NEWS-PRESS START EDITORIAL CAMPAIGN TO GET STATE DEPARTMENT TO PAY FOR KAREN WITHERS. BELIEVE SHE IS IN TERRIBLE DANGER. MONDELLO IS A KILLER.

The *News-Press* apparently believed me. I filed some pretty grim stories that helped too. I described Mondello as a cutthroat murderer who had killed over one hundred people and a man who "raped at will."

192

It was this last phrase that probably did the trick.

The *News-Press* demanded editorially that the State Department pay the ransom. The cry was taken up by other papers throughout the country.

The pressure was so great that a spokesman for the State Department called a special press conference and read a statement. "Despite pressure from many sources and the fact that the State Department is in full sympathy with the mother of Karen Withers, we are not authorized to use any funds to pay the ransom of an American citizen kidnaped in a foreign country. It would only set a precedent and lead to the kidnapings of other American citizens abroad."

In the meantime, I had tipped off the *News-Press* that William was in New York and, since he had been kidnaped by Mondello, he would make a good feature.

Simpson located him and printed a story about him.

He was immediately invited to appear on various television shows.

William found himself in the spotlight.

He insisted Karen's life was in danger and said he believed the ransom should be paid.

"If I was the American people," William said on the Ed Sullivan show, "I would start a fund for Karen Withers."

Ed Sullivan took a ten-dollar bill out of his pocket and said, "Let me be the first to contribute."

Hundreds of people sent in contributions to CBS, who turned them over to William.

The Fund for Karen Withers was born and William was made chairman.

Back at La Coma, Bartlett was organizing his own rescue team.

The hunchback didn't know Bartlett wasn't in on the plot and one morning, when he met him, he said, "The girl's all right."

Bartlett realized the hunchback knew where she was and said, "I want to see her."

The hunchback said it was too dangerous to have too many visitors.

Bartlett talked the hunchback into making a map for him, showing how to get to Mondello's headquarters. He said he would go there alone.

The hunchback reluctantly made the map. "I guess since she's your woman it's all right."

With the map, Bartlett sought out Pasquale. I saw them talking together by the church and wandered over.

"I'm going to get Karen," Bartlett said. "You want to come?"

"How are you going to find her?"

"The hunchback gave me a map of the area."

I was frightened. "It's too dangerous," I said.

"I don't care," Bartlett said. "I can do it."

He turned to Pasquale. "What do you say, Pasquale?" Bartlett said. "If you save the girl, they'll make you the chief of police of Palermo."

"Mondello would be very angry," Pasquale said.

"Yes, but think of what would happen to you. You would be the hero of the United States. Your name would go down in history with George Washington, Abraham Lincoln and Joe DiMaggio. If you're afraid of Mondello's revenge, I'll see you become a policeman in America. Then he would not be able to touch you."

"Could you really make me a policeman in the United States?" Pasquale asked.

"Of course," Bartlett said. "And remember this. In the United States, policemen don't ride on bicycles; they ride in cars."

"In automobiles?"

"With sirens and a red spotlight."

Pasquale's eyes opened. "A siren and a red spotlight?"

Bartlett slapped him on the back. "Pasquale, you've got the stuff that policemen are made of. Now listen closely. We need guns, blankets and horses. Are you coming, Pete?"

"No," I said. "I don't think so."

"You yellow bastard," Bartlett said. "I'll see you tonight, Pasquale."

Bartlett left us standing there.

"I don't want to go," Pasquale told me.

"Don't forget the siren and the spotlight," I said.

A letter had been found on the church steps and people were shouting. It was from Karen and it read, "Please help me. I'm all right but if the ransom isn't paid soon I don't know what will happen. Karen Withers."

The town was filling up with newspapermen and photographers from all over Europe. The beds of the men who were in prison were now rented out to the reporters. The Principessa filled up all her rooms at outrageous prices and Vincent had to hire two bartenders to take care of his business.

I knew that the State Department had turned down the ransom, but I was hoping the Fund for Karen Withers would be successful.

William had managed to raise $30,000 but was short $45,000. What he did, I later discovered, was to go to the organization and threaten that if they didn't contribute to the Karen Withers Fund, he would expose the real reason for her being in La Coma.

He said if he sang, the heat would really be on the organization.

They wanted to kill him on the spot, but William said he had already written the story and deposited it in a safe spot.

When Rizzolli heard the boys had given Bartlett a girl as a present, he got so angry that he told them they had to raise the money just to teach them a lesson.

Reluctantly, Bartlett's former mob sent wires all over the country, and bookies, gamblers, union treasurers and numbers racketeers were all told to contribute to the fund.

In forty-eight hours, William had the full $75,000. The fund for Karen Withers had been subscribed.

He appeared on the Ed Sullivan show again to announce the results. With him was a Pan American Airways captain. Pan American had agreed to fly the money to Palermo.

William promised he would deliver the money to Mondello himself. There was a great deal of applause in the audience as Sullivan bade him godspeed.

But as William left the theater with the Pan American captain, he was stopped by two men from the Treasury Department.

They wanted the money.

"You don't have a license to collect money for charity," they told him. "And with your record, we doubt if you'd ever get one. You'll have to return the money to the people you got it from."

William protested that he couldn't return it.

"In that case," they said, "we'll take it until it's legally disposed of."

William said, "What about the girl? This was going to pay her ransom."

"That isn't our problem. Our problem is the money. It can't leave the country. Let's have it."

The photographers took pictures of William handing over the satchel to the Treasury Department.

When the organization saw the pictures the next morning, they immediately went gunning for William.

I received word the next afternoon that the Karen Withers Fund had fallen through. It was the final blow.

There was no sense in having Karen held by Mondello any longer. It had been ten days since she had been taken. I told the hunchback I wanted to go to Mondello's that night. I had to call the whole thing off.

I sneaked out of La Coma late that night, and after taking a circuitous route to foil anyone who was following me, I went to the spot by the Madonna. I had to wait until three o'clock in the morning before someone came to guide me to the hideout. I didn't know what I would find when I got there, but it was certainly nothing that I had expected.

When I got to the hideout, Karen and Mondello were playing miniature golf! They were using the clubs that Mondello had stolen from Bartlett, and they had built a small golf course in the clearing.

"Did you get the money?" she cried when she saw me.

"No," I said, and then explained what had happened. "It's no use, Karen. It was a good idea but it didn't work."

Karen turned away and I explained the situation to Mondello.

He also was very sad. "Now she will have to go?"

"I'm afraid so. For your safety as well as hers."

"I'll leave tomorrow," Karen said. "I've cooked up a surprise for the boys tonight. Come see my cabin."

I walked over to the cabin with her. All her stolen trunks were there. "Giuseppe gave them back to me. Wasn't that wonderful?"

"What have you been doing here?" I asked.

"We've had a lot of laughs," Karen said. "We played golf. I taught them how and they love it. And we sang Italian songs and Giuseppe made me promise to find him a wife in America. My Italian is perfect and I've had a wonderful time. But now it's all spoiled by the news of the ransom. Oh, Pete, everything was going so well!"

"You don't realize what a storm you've kicked up around the world," I told her. "It's unbelievable. There must be two hundred reporters in La Coma. There are troops out looking for you, and Italian-American relations are at their lowest ebb."

"How's Frank?"

"Didn't he ever get here? He left three nights ago with Pasquale to rescue you."

"He never got here."

"He's probably lost somewhere in the woods. We'd better send out a rescue party."

"Nothing's gone right," Karen said.

"What's the surprise tonight?"

"You'll see. Leave me alone now. I want to pack . . . and cry."

Mondello came over and asked me if I wanted to play a game of golf. I said I didn't. I asked if I could sleep for a while. He let me use his pad, which was located inside the cool cave.

"Where does this cave lead?" I asked him.

Mondello grinned. "Through to the other side of the mountain."

I woke up around seven in the evening. Mondello had prepared a special farewell feast in honor of Karen. The men had roasted a pig and produced wine and we sat around the fire eating and drinking and enjoying ourselves.

# 20

THERE was a great deal of excitement around the fire while we all waited for Karen's surprise.

Suddenly she came out of the shack. I almost fell off my log. She was wearing the gold lamé dress she had worn the first night on the ship.

Mondello and his men gasped. Before anyone could make a move, Mondello picked up his rifle and aimed it at the men in case they made a move toward Karen.

One of Mondello's men kept rubbing his eyes.

Another muttered, "Mamma mia."

"Karen," I yelled. "You'll catch cold."

Karen walked toward the fire and we made room for her.

She bowed and we all applauded. Then she said in her sweet Italian, "Tonight I will sing all the songs from *My Fair Lady*, an American operetta in which I starred."

I started to cough, but Karen ignored me.

The men watched in fascination as she sang "Wouldn't

It Be Loverly?" Karen had a weak voice, but in those mountains on a night like this, Renata Tebaldi wouldn't have sounded as wonderful.

Although the men didn't understand the lyrics, they cheered wildly. Karen started singing "I Could Have Danced All Night." One of Mondello's men tried to get up, but Mondello pushed him down roughly.

Karen was singing "Why Can't a Woman Be More Like a Man?" when a shot rang out. Karen's voice, in the middle of a note, trailed off into a scream.

A voice yelled out of the blackness, "Don't anyone move!"

Mondello tried to pick up his gun, but another shot rang out and he dropped it.

"Do that again and you're dead," the voice said. I suddenly realized it was Bartlett.

"Karen," I said. "It's Frank."

"Frank," yelled Karen. "Don't shoot!"

Two men walked out of the shadows. Bartlett was carrying two pistols and Pasquale a submachine gun.

Mondello's men automatically put their hands up. It was such a funny picture I had to laugh. "Where have you been, Frank?"

"We got lost," Bartlett said. "Karen, did he hurt you?"

"Who told you to come here?" Mondello demanded.

Bartlett went over and slapped him in the face.

"Don't you hit Giuseppe," Karen cried.

"Giuseppe?" Bartlett said, turning to Karen. "What kind of talk is that? And what are you doing in that dress?"

"Giuseppe is my friend and has done me a great service.

I'm wearing this dress to repay him for the wonderful time he has shown me."

Bartlett's eyes flashed. "Why, you tramp!"

"Don't you call me a tramp," Karen cried. "Who asked you to come here anyway?"

"I didn't wait to be invited. I thought I might rescue you. Isn't that enough?"

"I don't want to be rescued! When I want to be rescued, I'll let you know."

"Did he drug you?" Bartlett said.

"Oh, go away," Karen said.

"I don't care if you want to be rescued or not. I'm taking in Mondello. There's a large price on his head. Maybe it will be enough to pay the fine."

"You leave Giuseppe alone, you big lug," Karen shouted. "And leave this camp right away!"

I thought it was about time someone explained what was happening. "Frank, let me tell you what's going on."

Bartlett whirled on me. "I don't need any explanations from you. Nothing's gone right since you've been around. I don't know what the hell you're doing here. As a matter of fact, I don't know what I'm doing here."

Bartlett turned back to Mondello. "Come on. Let's go, Giuseppe. I never turned anyone in before, but I'm going to enjoy this."

Karen ran up to Bartlett and started hitting him on the chest. "Leave Giuseppe alone, I said! Don't you understand we don't want you? You're just complicating everything."

"What about the fine?" Bartlett said, trying to parry the blows.

"We can't pay it by turning in Giuseppe," Karen said, and then she started to scream. "Please, go away! I'm doing this for you. We've got to help the people of La Coma. I asked Giuseppe to kidnap me."

Bartlett said, "What right have you to ask anyone to kidnap you? And who asked you to help me? I don't need a woman to fight my battles."

"You sure needed somebody," I said.

"Let me take Giuseppe in," Bartlett pleaded with Karen. "If only for my self-respect."

"No," said Karen. "You don't understand. It's no good that way. Giuseppe is risking his life for La Coma. He didn't want to kidnap me. I forced him to do it."

"I don't understand," Bartlett said.

"Leave us alone," Karen begged. "Go away. Don't you understand that?"

Pasquale asked, "What's the matter?"

"She doesn't want to be rescued," Bartlett said bitterly.

"And Mondello?"

"She doesn't want us to take him in."

"Women are crazy," Pasquale said.

"Damn right they're crazy," Bartlett said. "Come on, Pasquale, we're taking him in."

Karen picked up a gun off the ground. "Frank Bartlett, if you touch Giuseppe Mondello, I will shoot you."

"Put down that gun," Bartlett said.

"Yes," said Mondello, "please. I would rather die than be saved by a woman."

"Frank," I said. "Please go away. You're only causing trouble. We can't let you take in Mondello. I'll bring Karen back to La Coma in the morning, I promise."

Bartlett looked at me, then at Karen, and finally at Mondello. He threw down his pistols in disgust. "I never saw so many sick people in my life."

"But, Signor Bartelini, aren't we going to take him in?"

"What's the use? We'll only make a widow out of her."

"My job on the New York Police Force," Pasquale moaned. "My automobile."

Bartlett had already disappeared into the darkness. Pasquale ran after him, shouting, "Americans are crazy people!"

Karen ran into the shack and I could hear her sobbing.

The show was over. Poor Karen, I thought . . . poor Bartlett, and then, as an afterthought, poor Pete.

In the morning, we were ready to leave. Mondello was very sad. "I will miss you, Karen," he told her.

"I'll miss you, Giuseppe. You're the nicest bandit I'll ever know."

"Don't forget to send me the wife."

"I'll try," Karen promised.

We heard a long shrill whistle. It came from down a trail where Mondello had posted lookouts after Bartlett left.

Then we heard shooting.

Mondello shouted orders to the men. The men grabbed their horses and pulled them over to a trail. They hit them on the rumps and the horses ran down the path.

Then the men grabbed up their packs and the food and headed for the cave.

"Give Ruffino my regards," Mondello shouted as he

kissed Karen's hand. He shook my hand and disappeared into the cave.

Fifteen minutes later, Ruffino and ten of his troops charged into the clearing, their guns drawn.

He found Karen and me loosely bound up.

"Inspector Ruffino," I said. "I'm so glad you came. I finally found Karen."

One of Ruffino's men rushed over to the trail where the horses had been released. "They went this way," he called.

The others followed, except for Ruffino, who put his gun away and looked angrily at us.

"Oh, Inspector, you rescued me. How can I ever thank you? The American Government will be so pleased."

Ruffino snarled, "I might even get a promotion."

"When I write my story, you are going to get full credit," I told him.

"Thanks," Ruffino said. "I suggest Miss Withers put some dirt on her face or it's going to be hard to believe she went through so much hell."

"You're right, Inspector," she said. "I think I ought to tear my clothes, too. Do you both mind turning around?"

Karen started ripping the hem of her dress.

"I'm going to have you thrown out of Italy," Ruffino said to me.

"You were the one who reported Karen was kidnaped, Inspector. It would be very hard for you to explain it, if it weren't true. Let's leave well enough alone. You're a hero and Miss Withers is unharmed."

"I'll get Mondello someday," Ruffino vowed.

Karen had gotten herself pretty dirty. Her dress was torn and she had mussed up her hair.

The men came back. "They got away."

"How do I look now, Inspector?" Karen said.

I said, "You look like a beautiful, ravished victim of a Mondello kidnaping."

"Pete, you flatter me. Inspector, as long as your men have nothing better to do, would they take my bags back into town?"

Ruffino was muttering curses under his breath. He ordered the men to bring up their horses and load the bags.

"And don't forget Frank's golf clubs," Karen said.

We all started back into town.

At the outskirts of La Coma, people recognized Karen and shouted, "She's back! She's back!"

We rode into the square, where we were immediately surrounded by crowds of people, reporters and photographers.

Karen sat on her horse, crying, not because she had returned, but because she had failed to raise the money.

Reporters were shouting questions at her but she shook her head, sobbing. I pushed through them and led her into Vincent's and up to my room. She collapsed on the bed.

There was a knock on the door.

"Who is it?" I said.

"It's Rinaldo Renari of *Oggi*," a man shouted through the door. "We will pay you five hundred thousand lire for your story of the kidnaping of Mondello."

"Go away," I said.

I could hear arguing and shouting on the outside. Then someone shoved a piece of paper under the door. I picked it up and read it: "*Life* Magazine will pay you $20,000."

Another note was slipped under the door. "King Features—$30,000."

"Karen," I said. "They want to pay you for your kidnaping story."

Karen stopped sobbing and sat up in bed. I showed her the notes.

"Thirty thousand dollars!" she said.

Another note was shoved under the door. "The *Daily Sketch* will pay you £15,000."

"That's forty-five thousand dollars," I said to Karen.

I heard pounding on the door. "Pete, Pete. It's Boyle. Let me in."

I opened the door, and Boyle, the syndicate manager of the *News-Press*, squeezed in. I locked it again.

He pumped my hand. "Pete, my boy, I'm proud of you. We've got three hundred papers waiting for the series. We're going to make journalistic history. This kidnaping is worth ten Frank Bartlett stories. Did he rape her?" Boyle said hopefully.

"How much are you willing to pay, Boyle?" I said.

"Pay? Don't worry, Pete. We'll give you a bonus."

"I mean for Karen's story. The last offer was forty-five thousand dollars."

"Are you crazy, Pete? We don't have to pay her. You can write the story."

"It will cost you fifty thousand," I said.

"Fifty thousand dollars," Boyle yelled. "For what?" he shouted. "The *News-Press* sent you here, they've paid your expenses and your salary. Don't haggle with me."

"I'm sorry, Boyle," I said. "But this is an exclusive story. No one will pay Karen if we print it."

"Who cares about her? Write your version," Boyle said. "What are you trying to do?"

More notes were being shoved under the door.

"The syndicate can afford fifty thousand," I said. "You'll still make a profit on it."

"Pete, I'm giving you one more chance. Are you going to write this series on the kidnaping for us? If you say no, I'll have you fired, and what's more, there isn't a publisher in the United States who will hire you after a trick like this."

Karen said, "Pete, please write it. You'll ruin your whole career."

I picked up the other slips of paper off the floor.

"I might as well make a few sacrifices for La Coma too."

"You're through, Pete," Boyle yelled. "Through for good. Let me out of here."

I unlocked the door and let him out.

"Where's the guy from *Life*?" I called.

A man pushed his way through the crowd and I let him in.

"Are you paying fifty thousand for her story?"

"That's what the last note said," he replied.

"Have you got the check with you?"

"Right here in my pocket. I'll make it out now. Who should I make it out to?"

"Frank Bartlett," I said.

"Are you kidding?"

"Just do as I tell you."

He gave me the check and Karen signed the contract.

I went over to the window and saw Pasquale mingling with the crowd.

"Pasquale," I shouted. "Tell Mr. Bartelini Miss Withers has to see him right away. She's very sick."

The *Life* man left, and ten minutes later Bartlett rushed in. Karen ran into his arms. They kissed and then Karen explained the entire story and showed Bartlett the check.

"After you pay the fine, we can get married," Karen said.

"Married?"

"Yup," said Karen, laughing and crying at the same time.

"But if you marry me," Bartlett said, "you may have to stay in La Coma for the rest of your life."

"I don't care," said Karen. "I like La Coma."

"Of course," said Bartlett, "it doesn't always have to be like this. With organization and some know-how, we could make La Coma another Taormina."

"Or Capri," Karen said.

"We could build a gambling casino up on the hill."

"The fishermen could take tourists tuna fishing," Karen said.

"You could get Mondello to pose for post cards," I said. "Cut him in on the profits."

"We could have guided tours of the Principessa's castle," Karen said.

"And we could get the Frasconis to blast a hole down by the sea, paint it blue, and call it the Blue Grotto," Bartlett added.

Karen kissed Bartlett again and then said, "Darling, tell the people about the fine."

We walked over to the window and the crowds in the square gathered out in front.

Bartlett waved the check and shouted, "I'm going to pay the fine. Your men will be home by tomorrow."

The women in the square screamed with joy.

"And they'll get their boats back."

The women screamed again.

Just then, a donkey cart came into the square. Seated next to the driver was William. He was in his underwear.

This time the women screamed in anger.

"William!" Karen shouted.

William saw us at the window.

Looking up as he walked toward Vincent's café, he yelled at us.

"The son-of-a-bitch did it to me again!"

**Position Wanted** — Ex-crime reporter, very young, single, desires position with newspaper or public relations firm. Experienced writer. Speaks fluent Italian. Write Box 234D.

*Set in Caledonia*
*Format by Seamus Byrne*
*Manufactured by The Haddon Craftsmen, Inc.*
*Published by Harper & Brothers, New York*